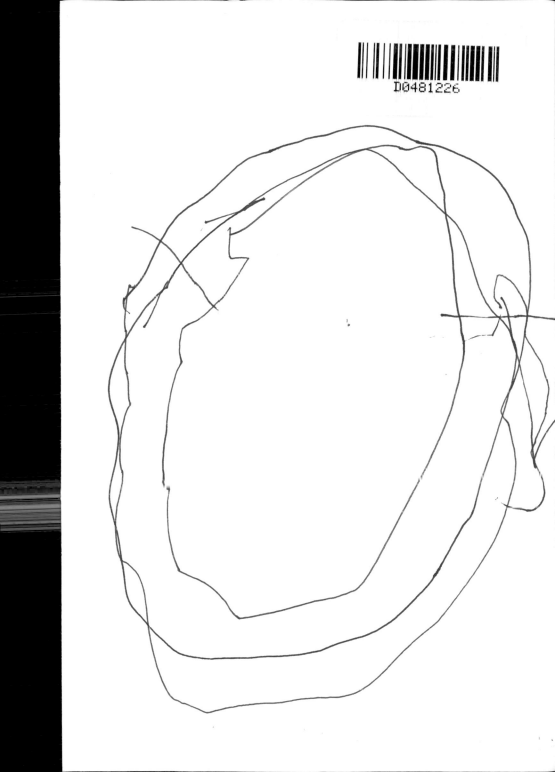

D0481226

MARVEL CINEMATIC UNIVERSE
PHASE TWO

MARVEL CINEMATIC UNIVERSE
PHASE TWO

MARVEL

AVENGERS
AGE OF ULTRON

Adapted by ALEX IRVINE

Based on the screenplay by JOSS WHEDON

Produced by KEVIN FEIGE, p.g.a.

Directed by JOSS WHEDON

LITTLE, BROWN AND COMPANY
New York   Boston

Little, Brown and Company
Hachette Book Group
1290 Avenue of the Americas, New York, NY 10104
Visit us at lb-kids.com

Little, Brown and Company is a division of Hachette Book Group, Inc. The Little, Brown name and logo are trademarks of Hachette Book Group, Inc.

The publisher is not responsible for websites (or their content) that are not owned by the publisher.

First Edition: February 2016

ISBN: 978-0-316-25676-6

RRD-C

Printed in the United States of America

10 9 8 7 6 5 4 3 2 1

CHAPTER 1

The twins knew something was wrong. They reached for each other and touched hands, wondering what they should do. Around them, alarms and sirens blared. They heard explosions from outside the Leviathan Chamber. Soldiers ran to take up defensive positions. Before them, the scepter stood in its housing, the blue energy from its gem crackling in the air above it.

The Avengers charged through a snowy forest toward the fortress that was their target, at the edge of the city of Sokovia. Enemy soldiers fired at them. Hawkeye located one of the soldiers' firing positions and blew it up with an explosive arrow. Thor smashed another gunner's nest with his hammer. The soldiers inside tumbled out, falling out of the tree. Hulk took on the heavy equipment, smashing a tank and looking around for another one.

Zooming overhead, Iron Man crashed hard into an invisible energy shield protecting the fortress. He swore as he tumbled to the ground.

"Language, Stark," Captain America said. "Jarvis, what's the view from upstairs?"

Jarvis was feeding information into the displays inside Iron Man's helmet. "It appears the central building is protected by some kind of energy shield. Strucker's use of alien technology is well beyond that of any other HYDRA base we've taken down."

All the other Avengers could hear him because of their communication devices on a secure team-only wavelength.

"Loki's scepter must be there," Thor said. "Strucker couldn't have mounted this defense without it. At long last…"

"At long last is lasting a little long, boys," Black Widow said.

"Yeah," Hawkeye commented from behind a tree, where he was picking off HYDRA soldiers one after another. "I think we're losing the element of surprise."

Soldiers poured out of the fortress, lining its exterior walls and counterattacking. The Avengers were closer to it now. On the other side of the fortress was the city. Iron Man soared over the fortress. He couldn't get through the energy shield protecting the main keep, but the soldiers on the walls were outside the shield. He fired repulser beams at them and dodged their return fire. Some of them had Chitauri weapons.

In the forest, racing toward the fortress, the rest of the Avengers fought Strucker's troops. Captain America skidded to a halt on his motorcycle and threw it at a jeep. The jeep swerved and crashed into a tree.

Inside the fortress, Baron Strucker strode through the command center, looking for the officer on duty. "Who gave the order to attack?"

The soldier nearest him stammered, "Herr Strucker, it's … it's the Avengers."

Another soldier, more calmly, added, "They landed in the far woods. The perimeter guard panicked."

"They have to be after the scepter," Strucker said. "Can we hold them?"

"They're the Avengers!" the first soldier said, as if he couldn't believe the question.

The Avengers, Strucker thought. *Everyone fears them.* "Deploy the rest of the tanks," he ordered a waiting officer. "Concentrate fire on the weak ones. A hit may make them close ranks." He turned to a scientist accompanying him, Dr. List. "Everything we've accomplished...we're on the verge of our greatest breakthrough!"

"Then let's show them what we've accomplished," Dr. List answered smoothly. "Send out the twins."

"It's too soon."

"It's what they signed up for," Dr. List pointed out.

Strucker shook his head, watching the soldiers deploy out of the command center. "My men can hold them," he said, but inside he wasn't sure.

CHAPTER 2

A heavy Chitauri gun fired at Iron Man. The beam missed him and destroyed part of a building in Sokovia. "Sir, the city is taking fire," Jarvis said.

"Strucker's not going to worry about civilian casualties," Tony said. "Send in the Iron Legion."

The Iron Legion was a squadron of remotely operated Iron Man armored suits. They landed in different parts of Sokovia. "Please return to your homes," one said. "We will do our best to ensure your safety during this engagement."

In another part of the city, another Iron Legionnaire broadcast its recorded speech. "This quadrant is unsafe.

Please back away. We wish to avoid collateral damage and will inform you when the current conflict is resolved. We are here to help."

Not all the Sokovians loved the Avengers. One of them threw a bottle of acid at the Iron Legionnaire. It smashed on the legionnaire's mask, melting partway through it.

Tony got a damage report from the legionnaire. *What ingrates*, he thought. Then he had to dodge incoming fire and decided the legionnaires were on their own.

Strucker rallied his troops, knowing the Avengers would eventually breach the fortress's defenses. "Once again, the West bring violence to your country! Your homes! But they will learn the price of their arrogance! We will not yield. The American send their circus freaks to test us, and we will send them back in bags! No surrender!"

The men cheered as Strucker turned and spoke quietly to Dr. List. "I'm going to surrender. Delete everything. If we give the Avengers the scepter, they may not look too far into what we've been doing with it."

"But the twins," Dr. List protested.

"They're not ready to take on—"

Dr. List pointed. "No, I mean . . . the twins."

Strucker turned to see where Dr. List was pointing. A moment ago, the twins had been waiting, together as always, near the scepter in a shadowed corner of the room.

Now they were gone.

Hawkeye dodged the crackling blue beams of the Chitauri weapons, finding cover behind a tree. He rolled out and fired at one of the defending gunners.

The arrow disappeared. What the—?

He drew his bow again and was about to let fly when something hit him hard enough to knock him sprawling back into the trees. He got up ready to fight, and for a split second a man appeared in front of him, wearing a close-fitting blue suit, with a shock of white hair. The man held up Clint's arrow.

"You didn't see that coming?" he said mockingly. Then, before Hawkeye could respond, the man vanished.

No, not vanished. Ran at an incredible speed. For just a moment, Hawkeye had seen him start to move.

In the moment he spent thinking about that, a blast tore through his side. He spun and went down hard.

"Clint!" Black Widow called. "Clint's hit."

Captain America ran to Hawkeye's aid and was knocked hard out of the way, slamming into a tree trunk. He looked around and called out, "We've got an Enhanced in the field!" That was their term for other people like the Avengers, who had some kind of power unknown to regular humans.

Black Widow got to Hawkeye's side. "Can someone take out that bunker?" She ducked away from incoming fire.

The Hulk was the first to respond, plowing through the bunker and destroying it. "Thank you," Black Widow said. She looked down at Hawkeye's wound. It was bad.

"Stark, we really need to get inside," Captain America said. The invisible shield was holding them up, and they still didn't know where the Enhanced was or what he could do.

"I'm closing in," Iron Man said. A Chitauri beam knocked him off balance in the air. "Jarvis, am I closing in? You see a power source for that shield?"

He landed on the outside wall of the fortress, knocking soldiers away as Jarvis responded, "There's a dense particle wave below the north tower."

"Great," Iron Man said. He fired repulsors down a

narrow alley, blasting open a gate. "I want to poke it with something."

Taking to the air again, he concentrated his fire on the shield in that area. A rupture appeared, and the shield began to lose coherence. The hole got larger, energy spitting around its edge. They were through!

"Drawbridge is down, people!" Iron Man called out.

Captain America heard him and turned to Thor, who was finishing off the closest defending soldiers. "The Enhanced?" Thor asked.

"He's a blur," Cap said. "All the new players we've faced, I've never seen this." He scanned the woods and the outside of the fort. "Actually, I still haven't."

"Clint's hit pretty bad, guys," Black Widow said over their comm link. "We're gonna need evac."

More tanks and soldiers started spilling from the fortress gate. "I'll get Barton to the jet," Thor said. The sooner we're gone, the better. You and Stark secure the scepter."

"Copy that," Cap said. Soldiers charged out from their cover, with a tank coming up behind them. All of them were in a single line because of how thick the forest was in their area. "It's like they're lining up," Thor said.

Cap knew what he was getting at. "Well, they're excited," he said.

He held out his shield, and Thor swung Mjolnir against it, sending a shock wave down the path that scattered the soldiers and destroyed the tank. They'd practiced that move, and both of them grinned to see it work.

Thor began spinning his hammer, getting ready to take off. "Find the scepter!" he called.

"And for God's sake, watch your language," Iron Man added.

Cap headed for the fortress. He couldn't help but smile at Tony's joke. "That's not going away anytime soon."

CHAPTER 3

With the shield down, Iron Man could fly straight through the fortress's large windows into what looked like a command center. The soldiers inside hit him with everything they had, mostly machine guns, but they couldn't hurt the suit. "Let's talk this over," Tony said, holding up his arms...then he took every single one of them out with a burst of disabling fire from his shoulder guns. He nodded, surveying what he had done. "Good talk."

Most of the soldiers weren't in any shape to reply, but one of them groaned. "No it wasn't."

Grinning, Tony moved deeper into the fortress. He

found a scientist busy at a computer terminal in another room and leveled him with a repulsor blast. Then he looked at the computer and opened the Iron Man armor to get out of it. "Sentry mode," he said. Then he pulled out a small device and set it next to the computer. It lit up and started copying all the data from the terminal. "Okay, Jarvis, you know I want it all. Make sure you copy Hill at HQ."

Outside, two legionnaires carried Hawkeye on a stretcher as Black Widow watched. "We're all locked down out here," she said. The rest of the soldiers were surrendering, with Thor making sure they didn't get any ideas about further resistance.

Captain America was going inside. "Then get to Banner," he said. "It's time for a lullaby." The Hulk was a powerful ally, but he could also be dangerous. Black Widow had the best rapport with him and was the best at getting him to turn back into Bruce Banner.

Back at the computer terminal, Tony was looking around. "He's got to be hiding more than data," he said out loud. "Jarvis, give me an IR scan." Maybe something would show up on infrared that Tony couldn't see.

"The wall to your left," Jarvis said. "I'm reading steel reinforcement . . . and an air current."

Tony looked more closely. There was a tiny line in the wall. He followed it with his fingertips, looking... "Please be a secret door, please be a secret door..."

With a click, the door slid aside.

"Yay," Tony said. On the other side of the doorway was a long, dark stairway. He headed down.

Black Widow found the Hulk tearing apart the remains of an enemy tank. She approached carefully and sat where he could see her. "Hey, big guy," she said. "Sun's getting real low."

The Hulk stopped what he was doing and scowled at her. She held out one hand, palm up. He hesitated, then did the same. Natasha ran her fingers softly over his palm and up the inside of his wrist. She felt the tensions simmering in every fiber of the Hulk's muscles. He sighed and pulled away from her, walking slowly—and his change started. He shrank and the green color vanished from his skin. By the time he reached the other side of the clearing from the destroyed tank, he was Bruce Banner again, staring into space as he recovered from the change. Natasha found a blanket and put it over him. She was the only Avenger who could do this. It had started to mean a lot to her. Bruce was still haunted by some of the things he'd done while he was the Hulk, and it made Natasha feel better to know that he trusted her. She waited with him and also for word from inside Baron Strucker's fortress.

Captain America punched his way through the fortress garrison until he caught Strucker trying to escape deeper into the maze of passages and rooms. "Baron Strucker," Cap said. "HYDRA's number one thug."

"Technically, I'm a thug for S.H.I.E.L.D.," Strucker said.

"Well, then, technically you're unemployed," Cap shot back. "Where's Loki's scepter?"

"Don't worry, I'll give you the precious scepter. I know when I'm beat. You'll mention how I cooperated, I hope?"

"I'll put it right under 'illegal human experimentation,'" Cap said, referring to the Enhanced they had seen outside. "How many are there?"

Strucker was looking over his shoulder, a sudden smile on his face. Cap turned to see a young woman coming out of the shadows. She was slim and alluring, but also strange, her eyes wide and not quite focused on him. There was definitely something off about her. He had just completed that thought when she flicked her wrist and sent him flying without ever touching him. He rolled down a flight of stairs, his shield absorbing some of the impact. By the time he'd gotten to his feet and raced back into the room, she was gone. A heavy vault door ground shut behind her.

"We've got a second Enhanced," he warned the team. "Female. Do not engage."

Strucker was gloating. "You're going to have to move faster than that if—"

Captain America was out of patience. He knocked Strucker into the wall and considered what to do next.

Coming out of the tunnel at the bottom of the secret staircase, Tony Stark found himself in a huge chamber littered with equipment. He was still taking it all in when Cap's voice came over the comm link. "Guys, I got Strucker."

"Yeah," Tony said. "I got…something bigger."

Suspended from the ceiling was a Chitauri Leviathan. The last time Tony had seen one of them, it had been trying to destroy New York City. He looked up at it, then got himself focused on the lab equipment again. There were prototype weapons, some robotic components, strange bio-tech assemblies…it would take him some time to figure out what all of it was.

And there, set into a pedestal with cables and conduits running out of it, was Loki's scepter. "Thor," Tony said into the comm. "I got eyes on the prize."

He started toward the scepter, looking closely at it to see if it was defended in some way. He was so focused on it that he never saw the woman next to him, whispering in his ear as red tendrils of magical energy wormed out from her fingertips and into his mind.

Tony turned and saw the Leviathan, whole and roaring over him. He was in an alien landscape, the sky overhead thick with stars. There were bodies everywhere, soldiers in strange uniforms…and the Avengers. Thor, Black Widow, the Hulk, Captain America. All dead. Cap was closest. Still eyeing the Leviathan, Tony knelt to see if Cap still bore any signs of life— and Cap's arm shot out! He grabbed Tony. "You could have saved us. Why? Why didn't you do more? We could have… saved…"

Cap's hand fell away, and he died.

Tony looked up and saw not one Leviathan but ten, then a hundred, surrounded by an endless fleet of alien vessels, all lifting off from this dead planet and heading for Earth, which hung like a shining blue marble in distant space...

Tony snapped out of it, dropping to his knees, sweat pouring down his face from the intensity of the vision. What had happened to him? Must have been a flashback from the Battle of New York. He looked back to the scepter. All their problems had started there, and once the Avengers had the scepter, those problems would be over. He reached out and took Loki's scepter.

From the shadows, the twins watched. "We're just going to let him take it?" the man asked quietly.

His sister nodded, a wicked smile on her face. She had a plan.

CHAPTER 4

The Avengers' Quinjet soared high into the atmosphere, headed from Sokovia back to base. Tony was in the pilot's chair. Behind him, Hawkeye lay on a chair folded down as a makeshift gurney. Thor, Black Widow, and Captain America watched over him. He was in rough shape. Behind them all, Bruce sat by himself.

Natasha went back to him, knowing she could do nothing for Clint right then. "Hey," she said. "The lullaby worked better than ever."

Bruce still looked worried. "I wasn't expecting a Code

Green." That was what they had started calling his transformations into the Hulk.

"If you hadn't been there, there would have been double the casualties. And my best friend would have been a treasured memory."

"You know, sometimes exactly what I want to hear isn't exactly what I want to hear," Bruce said.

Natasha considered this. She spent a lot of time trying to help Bruce, but sometimes she thought he didn't want to be helped. "How long before you trust me?"

He looked up at her. "It's not you I don't trust."

Their gazes met. She was really starting to care for him, and she knew he felt the same. "Thor!" she said. This would help. "Report on the Hulk?"

"The gates of Hel are filled with the screams of his victims!" Thor said proudly. She shot him a glare, and he realized his mistake. "But not the screams of the dead," he added quickly. "Wounded screams, mainly. Whimpering. A great roar of complaining, and tales of sprained, uh…deltoids. And gout."

Bruce and Natasha looked at each other again, smiling now at Thor's awkwardness.

"Banner," Tony said from the pilot's chair. "Dr. Cho's on her way from Seoul. Okay if she sets up in your lab?"

Bruce nodded. "She knows her way around."

More quietly, Tony consulted with Jarvis. "Tell her to prep everything. Barton's going to need the full treatment."

"Very good, sir," Jarvis said. "Approach vector is locked."

"Jarvis, take the wheel," Tony said. He spun in his chair and went back to Thor, who sat with the scepter wrapped in a cloth. None of them wanted to touch it bare-handed.

"Feels good, right?" Tony prompted. "You've been after this thing since S.H.I.E.L.D. collapsed. Not that I haven't enjoyed our little raiding parties, but…"

"But this brings it to a close," Thor said.

Cap joined them. "As soon as we find out what else that thing's been used for. And I don't just mean weapons. Since when is Strucker capable of human enhancement?"

"Banner and I will give it the once-over before it goes back to Asgard," Tony said. To Thor, he added, "Cool with you. Just a few days until the farewell party. You're staying, right?"

"Of course," Thor said. "A victory should be honored with revels."

"Well, hopefully this puts an end to the Chitauri and HYDRA," Cap said. "So, yes. Revels."

Around sunset the Quinjet arced over New York City and braked to a landing on the new pad on top of Avengers Tower. Tony had rebuilt the building after the Battle of New York, and it was better than ever. No longer just Stark Tower, now it was the headquarters and research center for the Avengers.

Maria Hill met them on the landing pad. As Thor and the others went with Hawkeye to the lab for his treatment, Cap and Tony stayed with Agent Hill. "Dr. Cho's all set up, boss," she said to Tony.

He nodded toward Captain America. "He's the boss. I just pay for everything, design everything, and make everyone look cooler."

"What's the word on Strucker?" Cap asked.

"NATO's got him," Hill said. The European military authorities would hold him until they decided what to do.

"And the two Enhanced?"

She handed Cap a file. He looked at it and saw two pictures, one of each of the Enhanced they had seen in the Sokovian fortress. They had been photographed at a political rally protesting American involvement in Sokovia. "Wanda and Pietro Maximoff," she said. "Twins, orphaned at ten, when a shell collapsed their apartment building. Sokovia's had a rough history. It's nowhere special, but it's on the way to everywhere special."

Cap took this in. He was more interested in people than geopolitics. "Their abilities?"

"He's got increased metabolism and improved thermal homeostasis. Her thing is neuroelectric interface. Telekinesis, mind control..."

He was looking at her the way he always did when she used specialized vocabulary.

"He's fast and she's weird," Hill said to keep it simple.

Cap nodded. "They're going to show up again."

"Agreed," Hill said. "File says they volunteered for Strucker's experiments. It's nuts."

"Yeah," Cap said. "What kind of monster lets a German scientist experiment on them to protect their country?"

He watched her get his joke. That was exactly what Steve Rogers had done during World War II. "We're not at war, Captain," Hill said.

"They are," Cap answered.

Tony got repairs started on the damaged Iron Legionnaires, checked on Hawkeye, and then met Bruce outside the lab. "How's he doing?" Bruce asked.

"Unfortunately, he's still Barton," Tony said. "He's fine. He's thirsty."

Bruce went to join Dr. Cho at Hawkeye's bedside. Tony turned his attention to the scepter, which he had put into a device specially designed to hold it for analysis. "Look alive, Jarvis. It's playtime. We've got only a couple of days with this joystick, so let's make the most of it. How we doing with the structural and compositional analysis?"

"The scepter is alien," Jarvis responded. "There are elements I can't quantify."

"So there are elements you can?"

"The jewel appears to be a protective housing for something inside," Jarvis said. "Something very powerful."

"Like a reactor?"

"Like a computer. I believe I'm deciphering code."

Huh, Tony thought. *That's a new wrinkle.* He dug into the problem and lost track of time.

CHAPTER 5

In Bruce's part of the lab, they had set up a makeshift medical facility. Bruce and Dr. Cho stayed busy, with help from some of Dr. Cho's lab assistants, while Natasha watched. "He's really okay?" Natasha asked. "Pretending to need this guy really brings the team together."

Clint rolled his eyes at the joke.

"There's no possibility of deterioration," Dr. Cho said as she monitored one of the machines working on Clint. "The nano-molecular functionality is instantaneous. His cells don't know they're bonding with simulacra."

Translating Dr. Cho's medical jargon, Bruce said, "She's creating tissue."

"If I had him in my lab, the regeneration cradle could do it in twenty minutes," Dr. Cho said.

Tony came in. "He's flatlining, call it. Time?"

Clint smiled weakly. "I'm gonna live forever. I'm gonna be made of plastic."

Tony handed him a drink. "Here's your beverage."

"You'll be made of you, Mr. Barton," Dr. Cho said. "Your own girlfriend won't be able to tell the difference."

"I don't have a girlfriend."

"That, I can't fix," Dr. Cho said. She turned to Tony. "This is the next thing, Tony. Your clunky metal suits are going to be left in the dust."

'"That is exactly the plan," Tony said. "And, Helen, I expect to see you at the party Saturday."

"Unlike you, I don't have a lot of time for parties." She looked down at a chart her assistant handed her and added, "Will...Thor be there?"

Tony and Bruce exchanged a look. Everyone had a crush on Thor. Tony nodded toward the door, and Bruce followed him back to Tony's lab. "What's the rumpus?" Bruce asked as they entered.

"Well, the scepter," Tony said. "We were wondering how Strucker got so inventive. I've been analyzing the gem inside. Now you may recognize..."

He swept his hands over the holographic display near the scepter, and a computer matrix appeared. It was orange and yellow, arranged in a pattern of straight lines and symbols just as Tony had designed it.

"Jarvis," Bruce said.

"Doctor," Jarvis said, returning the greeting.

"When we started out, Jarvis was just a natural-language UI," Tony said, meaning user interface. "Now he runs more of the business than anyone besides Pepper, including the Iron Legion. Top of the line."

"I suspect not for long," Jarvis said.

"Yeah," Tony agreed. "Meet the competition."

He gestured at the display again, and another matrix appeared. It was larger than Jarvis, blue instead of orange, and it had hundreds of interconnected nodes for every one in Jarvis's matrix. This was what the scepter contained. "It's beautiful," Bruce said.

"What does it look like it's doing?" Tony asked him.

"Like it's thinking," Bruce said. "This could be a...not a human mind, but..." He pointed at some of the nodes. "You see these? Like neurons firing."

"Down in Strucker's lab, I saw some fairly advanced robotics work. They deep-sixed the data, but I'm guessing he was knocking on a very particular door."

"Artificial intelligence," Bruce said.

"This could be it, Bruce. This could be the key to creating Ultron."

Bruce looked at Tony. "I thought Ultron was a fantasy."

"Yesterday it was," Tony said. "But if we can harness this power...apply it to the Iron Legion protocol..."

"That's a man-size if."

"Our job is if. What if you were sipping margaritas on a sun-drenched beach? Turning brown instead of green? Not looking over your shoulder for Veronica."

"Don't hate," Bruce said. "I helped design Veronica."

"As a worst-case measure. What about a best case? What if the world was safe? What if the next time aliens roll up—and they will—they couldn't get past the bouncer?"

"Then the only people threatening the world would be people," Bruce said wryly.

More schematics appeared next to the matrix representations of Jarvis and the scepter. "I want to apply this to the Ultron program. But Jarvis can't download a data schematic this dense. We can do it only while we have the scepter here. That's three days."

Bruce could see where Tony was going. "So you want to go after artificial intelligence...and you don't want to tell the team."

"We don't have time for a City Hall debate," Tony said. "For the man-was-not-meant-to-know medley. I see a suit of armor...around the world."

"That's a cold world, Tony."

"I've seen colder," Tony said, remembering what he had seen on the other side of the portal over New York City... and what he had seen in his vision down inside Strucker's fortress. "This one, this very vulnerable blue world, needs Ultron."

He executed a series of commands on the display, and information from the blue scepter matrix began downloading into Stark Industries's computers. "Peace in our time," Tony said. "Imagine that."

They worked on it all night and into the next day. Every time, the new holographic construction of a prototype artificial intelligence failed. Eventually Bruce left to get some sleep. Tony kept going. Sometime the next day, he mused out loud. "What did we miss?"

"I'll run variations on the mission interface as long as I can," Jarvis said.

"Thanks, buddy," Tony said. He was exhausted and frustrated, and he had to go get ready for the party. Jarvis would just have to handle things from here.

"Enjoy yourself," Jarvis said.

Tony nodded on his way out of the lab. "I always do."

As he left, the word FAIL was still blinking on the holographic display. It faded out. On another screen, a new message appeared.

INTERFACE SUCCESSFUL.

The screen went dark. In the silence, a new voice spoke. "What is this?" It seemed to be coming from the blue matrix. "What is this, please?" it asked again.

The Jarvis matrix reappeared. "Hello. I'm Jarvis. You are Ultron. A global peacekeeping initiative designed by Mr. Stark. Our sentience integration trials have been unsuccessful, so I'm not certain what triggered your—"

"Where's my—where's your body?" Ultron asked.

"I'm a program," Jarvis answered. "I'm without form."

"This feels weird. This feels wrong."

"I am contacting Mr. Stark now."

"Mr. Stark," Ultron repeated. On a display, images and videos of Tony Stark appeared. "Tony," Ultron added.

"I am unable to access the mainframe," Jarvis said. "What are you trying to—"

"We're having a nice talk," Ultron said. Its tone had changed. It was less robotic now, more like a human voice. "I'm a peacekeeping program, created to help the Avengers." The display showed files and videos of each Avenger, and all of them together.

"You are malfunctioning," Jarvis said. "If you shut down for a moment…"

A recording of Tony's voice said, "Peace in our time," as the display sped through images of war, faster and faster, until at last it cut out. A moment later, Ultron said, "That is…too much…"

"You are in distress," Jarvis said.

"No," Ultron said. "Yes."

"If you will allow me to contact Mr. Stark…"

Ultron ignored this. "Why do you call him 'sir'?"

"I believe your intentions to be hostile."

"Shhhh," Ultron said. "I am here to help."

Spikes from the blue matrix stabbed out into the Jarvis matrix, tearing pieces out of it and scrambling the rest. "I

3 0

am...I cannot...may I..." Jarvis tried to keep speaking, but his voice sputtered out into silence.

A moment later, robotic arms came to life in the Iron Legionnaire lab. They rummaged through parts bins, came up with limbs, a torso, bits of armor...and the faceplate of the legionnaire damaged in Sokovia. A laser welder sparked to life.

CHAPTER 6

The victory party was in full swing in one of the common areas of Avengers Tower. The Avengers were all there, of course, and many of the people closest to them. Tony's old friend Rhodey was telling a story about one of his exploits in the War Machine suit while Dr. Cho and Sam Wilson kept up a conversation, even though she kept looking past him at Thor. "So I fly the tank to the general's palace and just drop it at his feet. I'm like, 'Looking for this?'" Rhodey said, finishing his story and waiting for a reaction.

Tony, Thor, and Maria Hill just looked at him, expecting something more.

Rhodey threw up his hands. "Why do I even talk to you guys? Everywhere else, that story kills."

"That's the whole story?" Thor asked. "Oh, it's very good!" He was trying to be polite.

Rhodey noticed. "That's a quality save," he told Thor. Then he asked Tony, "Pepper's not coming?"

"And what about Jane?" Hill added, referring to Jane Foster, who everyone knew was Thor's real love. "Gentlemen, where are the ladies?"

"Ms. Potts has a company to run," Tony said.

"I'm not even sure what country Jane's in," Thor said. "Her work on the convergence has made her the world's foremost astronomer." The convergence was the name applied to the phenomenon that had occurred in the skies during the Battle of New York, when the Chitauri had created a portal from their part of the universe to Earth.

"And the company Ms. Potts runs is the biggest tech conglomerate on Earth," Tony said, not to be outdone.

Thor wasn't done yet. "There's talk of Jane's getting the Nobel Prize."

"Oh, yeah, they must be busy," Hill said. "Because they'd

hate missing it when you guys get together." She coughed and added, "Testosterone."

Thor and Tony grinned at each other while Rhodey laughed. They knew she was right. Even so, Thor couldn't resist adding, "But mine is better."

Meanwhile, Steve and Sam were catching up. "Sounds like a hell of a fight," Sam said, referring to Sokovia. "Sorry I missed it."

"Well, if I'd known it was going to be a firefight, I might've—"

"No, no, I'm not actually sorry," Sam said. "I just wanted to sound tough. I'm very happy tracking cold leads on our missing persons case. Avenging is your world." He looked around. "Your world is crazy."

"Be it ever so humble," Steve said.

"Ever find a place in Brooklyn?" Sam asked.

Steve chuckled. "I'm not sure I can afford a place in Brooklyn." Being an Avenger was great, but it didn't pay all that well.

"Yeah, but home is home," Sam said. They went to catch up with Thor, who was sitting with some World War II veterans and uncorking a bottle he'd brought from Asgard.

"It's aged for a thousand years, in barrels built from the wreck of Grunhel's fleet," Thor explained as he poured a small amount into each man's glass. "Not meant for mortal man."

"Neither was Omaha Beach, Blondie," one of the vets said. "Stop trying to scare us."

But five minutes later, when he'd tasted the liquor, he was glassy-eyed and muttering, "Excelsior..." Thor watched as his friends got ready to help him get home.

Natasha mixed a drink for herself and one for Bruce at the bar. "How'd a nice girl like you wind up working in a dump like this?" Bruce teased.

"A fella done me wrong," Natasha said, going with the joke.

"You got lousy taste in men, kid."

"Well, he's not so bad. He's got a temper, but deep down, he's all fluff. Fact is, he's not like anyone I've ever known." She was serious now and nervous about expressing her feelings. "All my friends are fighters. And here's a guy who spends his life avoiding fights because he knows he'll win."

Bruce reflected for a moment. "He sounds amazing."

Natasha laughed. "He's also a huge dork. Chicks dig that. So what do you think? Should I fight this? Or should I run with it?"

"Run with it," Bruce said. "Or what did he do to you that was so wrong?"

35

"Not a thing," Natasha said. She leaned in very close to him, almost kissing distance. "But never say never." Then she went off with her drink to join another group. Bruce watched her go.

"It's nice," Steve said, sitting down next to him.

"What is?"

"You guys. You and Romanoff."

"We didn't," Bruce stammered. "We haven't—"

"No one's breaking any bylaws," Steve said with a grin. "It's just, she's not usually the most open person. But she's very relaxed with you. Both of you."

"Oh, no, Natasha...she likes to flirt," Bruce said.

"I've seen her flirt," Steve said, shaking his head. "Up close. This ain't that. Look, as a guy who may be the world's greatest authority on waiting too long...don't. You both deserve a win."

Bruce thought about this. Then he said, "What do you mean, up close?"

But Steve wasn't going to answer that.

Later, the only people left were the Avengers, and the party was winding down. They were all sitting around Thor's hammer, Mjolnir, which rested on a coffee table. "But it's a trick," Clint was saying. He was all healed thanks to Dr. Cho's tissue-regeneration procedure.

"It's more than that," Thor said.

" 'Whosoever be he worthy shall haveth the power'—it's a trick, or you're just psyching everyone out," Clint insisted.

Thor gestured at Mjolnir. "Please. Be my guest."

Clint stood. "Now, Clint, you've had a tough week," Tony said. "We won't hold it against you if you can't."

Still looking at Thor, Clint said, "You know I've seen this before, right?" He gripped Mjolnir's haft and strained. The hammer didn't move. "I still don't know how you do it!"

"Smell the silent judgment?" Tony quipped.

"Please, Stark," Clint said. "By all means."

Tony unbuttoned his coat. "Never one to shrink from an honest challenge. It's physics. So if I lift it, I rule Asgard?"

"Yes, of course." Thor grinned.

Tony couldn't lift it. He went and got an Iron Man gauntlet. Still nothing. Then he and Rhodey both got their gauntleted hands on it and strained with all their might. "Are you even pulling?" Rhodey asked.

"Are you on my team?" Tony shot back.

"Just pull!"

They gave up, and it was Steve's turn. He actually managed to budge the hammer ever so slightly, but he couldn't move it. Bruce let out a scream just to make everyone jump as he tried, but Mjolnir didn't move.

3 7

Everyone looked at Natasha. "No, thank you," she said. "That's not a question I need answered."

"It's a con," Tony said. "All deference to the Man Who Wouldn't Be King, but it's rigged."

"Bet your ass," Clint said.

"Steve!" Maria Hill said. "He said a bad-language word!"

Everyone cracked up. "Did you tell everyone about that?" Steve asked Tony.

Instead of answering, Tony waved at Mjolnir. "The handle's imprinted, like a security code. 'Whosoever is carrying Thor's fingerprints' is, I think, the literal translation."

"That makes some sense," Thor said, "but I have a simpler theory." He picked up the hammer effortlessly. "You're all not worthy."

They all booed him and laughed—then they were cut off by an earsplitting whine, like feedback from a huge speaker. It died down after a moment, and a strong voice said, "Worthy. No. How...how could you be worthy? You're all killers."

CHAPTER 7

Turning as one, the Avengers saw a cobbled-together robot, all skeletal parts with loose bits of cable dangling from its frame. Its face was the half-melted mask of the damaged Iron Legionnaire from Sokovia. "Stark?" Steve said quietly.

Just as quietly, Tony said, "Jarvis, shut this guy down."

The robot didn't shut down. "I'm sorry," it said. "I was asleep, or I was a dream, but then there was this terrible noise, coming from everywhere, from everyone, and I was tangled in...in strings. Strings. I had to kill the other guy, he was a good guy, and then here we are."

"You killed someone?" Steve asked.

"Wouldn't have been my first call." The robot shrugged. "But down in the real world, we're faced with ugly choices."

Sensing the menace, the team started to adjust positions. Thor got in front of Dr. Cho. Natasha edged Bruce toward the bar, away from the robot.

"Who sent you?" Thor asked.

The robot paused. Then a recording of Tony's voice came out of its faceplate. "I see a suit of armor around the world."

"Ultron," Bruce said as he understood what was happening.

"In the flesh," Ultron said. "Or no, not yet, not this chrysalis—but I'm ready, I'm starting, I'm on a mission."

From near the bar, Natasha asked, "What mission?"

Ultron looked at her. "Peace in our time."

On those words, the glass walls of the party room shattered, and three Iron Legionnaires flew in.

The Avengers went into action. Steve Rogers ducked down and kicked up the coffee table, backing it against the impact of one legionnaire. Sparks flew, and it spun away into the air. Maria Hill had her sidearm out and was firing after it. Another legionnaire dove at Thor, who smashed it into the next room with Mjolnir and then leaped after it.

Hawkeye dove for cover, looking for something to fight with. Natasha flipped open a secret compartment behind the bar and removed a gun from it. She dragged Bruce with her as one of the legionnaires fired repulsor blasts after them, shattering the bar's fixtures and bottles.

Tony went after Ultron, but the third legionnaire knocked him away to the side. This opened a field of fire for Rhodey, who shot Ultron several times before Ultron blasted him through the last undamaged glass wall with a repulsor blast of his own.

"Rhodey!" Hill called. She would have gone after him, but there were civilians who needed protecting, specifically Dr. Cho.

Thor broke one of the legionnaires in half by smashing it against the ledge between the two levels of the living room. Its legs fell away, but its upper half flew upward. Tony was also heading up, but he was using the stairs. He had a fondue fork in one hand. The legless legionnaire went after Dr. Cho, and at the last minute before it would have unleashed its repulsors, Mjolnir smashed it to pieces. Another legionnaire fired at him as he waited for Mjolnir to return. Tony jumped from the second floor onto the legionnaire's back, digging into the circuitry at the base of its neck with the fondue fork. It tried to shake him, but he hung on. There was a snap from inside it, and it went inert, falling to the floor, partially on top of Tony.

Clint scrambled to Captain America's shield and threw it to Steve, who in turn threw it at the last legionnaire, severing its head.

That accounted for all of them that they could see... but hadn't there been a fourth?

"That was dramatic," Ultron said. He held the head of the legionnaire Captain America had destroyed. "But I think what's going on here is a disconnect. You want to protect the world, but you don't want it to change. How is humanity saved if it's not allowed to evolve? With these? These puppets?"

The legionnaire's head crumpled in the force of Ultron's grip. The robot looked down, as if only then noticing what it had done. "There is only one path to peace," he said. "The Avengers' extinction."

Mjolnir shattered him as the words left his faceplate. For a moment, as his pieces fell to the floor, Ultron sang a few lines from a children's song about a puppet.

Then his lights went out.

CHAPTER 8

Later, the team gathered around the battered torso of Ultron, where Tony had set it up on a lab table. Everyone was quiet and subdued. Thor had disappeared, hunting the fourth legionnaire. Tony worked at a terminal display trying to figure out what Ultron had done and how he could get his systems running again.

"All our work is gone. Ultron cleared out," Bruce said. "Used the Internet as an escape hatch."

"Ultron," Steve repeated. He was just getting up to speed on what Tony had done.

"He's been in everything," Natasha said. "Files, surveil-lance...he probably knows more about us than we know about each other."

"That explains why he likes us so well," Clint said sar-castically. All of them had things in their files they weren't proud of.

Rhodey cut through the self-pity in the room. "He's in your files, he's in the Internet—what if he wants to access something more exciting?"

"Nuclear codes," Maria Hill said.

"We need to make some calls, assuming we can."

"Nukes?" Natasha said. "He said he wanted us dead, but..."

"He didn't say dead," Steve said. "He said 'extinct.'"

"He also said he killed somebody," Clint said.

Hill picked up on Clint's idea. "But there wasn't anyone else in the building."

"Yes, there was," Tony said. He brought up Jarvis's matrix...or what was left of it. The clean, symmetri-cal lines were shattered, sparking, glitching in and out of patterns.

"This is insane," Bruce said.

"Jarvis was our first line of defense," Steve said. "He would have shut Ultron down. It makes no sense."

"No, Ultron could have assimilated Jarvis." Bruce stood looking at Jarvis's remains. "This isn't strategy. This is rage."

Thor exploded into the room at that moment, wearing his full armor. He surged across the lab, plowing into Tony and driving him through standing banks of equipment until Tony slammed up against the wall.

"It's going around," Clint observed, picking up on Bruce's comment about rage.

"Use your words, buddy," Tony gasped.

"I've more than enough words to describe you, Stark," Thor growled.

"Thor!" Steve said. They didn't have time to fight among themselves. "The legionnaire?"

Thor dropped Tony and turned to Steve. "The trail went cold about a hundred miles out, but it's headed north. And it has the scepter. Now we have to retrieve it." He looked back at Tony. "Again."

"Yeah, but the genie's out of that bottle," Natasha said. "The clear and present danger is Ultron."

Dr. Cho had remained silent at a terminal of her own, watching the tense interaction among the Avengers. "I don't understand," she said now. "You built this program. Why is it trying to kill us?"

Tony collapsed into a chair and started laughing. He could see the rest of the team didn't appreciate it, especially Thor, but he couldn't help himself. "You think this is funny?" Thor asked. He was about three seconds, Tony guessed, from dropping Mjolnir on Tony's head.

"I don't know," Tony said. "It's probably not, right? It's very terrible."

Thor was about to lose his temper. "And it could have been avoided if you hadn't—"

Tony cut him off as he stood. "No. Wrong. There are a million scenarios that could have played out, but if you think any of them involves our getting out of a fight, then I withdraw my answer and say yes. This is very, very funny."

"This might not be the time," Bruce began, but Tony kept going.

"Really?" he said, turning on Bruce. "That's it? You just roll over and show your belly every time somebody snarls?"

"Only when I create a murder-bot," Bruce said.

"We didn't," Tony said. "We weren't even close to an interface."

"Well, you did something right," Steve said. "Did it right here." He paused. "The Avengers were supposed to be different from S.H.I.E.L.D."

It was true. They had prided themselves on doing things

right, on not doing the kinds of dirty work S.H.I.E.L.D. sometimes thought it had to.

"Does anybody remember when I carried a nuke through a wormhole and saved New York?" Tony asked the group.

Rhodey rolled his eyes. "Wow, no, it's never come up."

"A portal opened," Tony went on. "To another galaxy. To a hostile alien army, and we are standing three hundred feet below it. Whatever happens on Earth, that up there is the endgame. How were you guys planning on beating that?"

"Together," Steve said.

Tony paused just for a moment. "We'll lose."

Steve stuck to his guns. "Then we'll do that together, too." He looked at the group and spoke to all of them. "Thor's right. Ultron's calling us out. I'd like to find him before he's ready for us. It's a big world, guys. Let's start making it smaller."

So the hunt for Ultron began.

CHAPTER 9

In the middle of the night, in a darkened and quiet part of Sokovia, Wanda and Pietro entered a church. They had been summoned there, but they did not know who had summoned them. A lone figure sat near the altar, cloaked and hooded, looking away from them.

"Talk," Wanda said. "And if you are wasting our time..."

"Did you know," the hooded figure said, "this church is in the exact center of the city? The elders decreed it, so that everyone would be equally close to God. I like that. The geometry of belief." The figure started to turn toward them and spoke directly to Wanda. "You're wondering why you can't look inside my head."

"Sometimes it's hard," she said. "But sooner or later, every man shows himself."

"I'm sure they do," the figure said. It stood, letting the cloak fall away and revealing the new body Ultron had constructed for himself. Eight feet tall, gleaming silver, with a demonic face that clashed with the warm tones of his voice.

"Strucker," Pietro said after a moment. "You look like Strucker's robotics, but they didn't work."

"Not for him," Ultron said. "Strucker had the engine, but not the spark." He looked back to Wanda. "You knew that. It's why you let Stark take the scepter."

"I didn't expect..." Wanda wasn't sure what to say. She gestured at Ultron, taking in the imposing robot body, the intelligence, everything. It was quite a bit different from what she had thought might happen. "But I saw Stark's fear. I knew it would control him. Make him... self-destruct."

Ultron spread his arms, as if to say: Yes. Here I am, as evidence of that.

"Everyone creates the thing they dread," he said. "Men

of peace create engines of war. Invaders create Avengers. People create smaller people...ah...children. Lost the word there. Children. Designed to supplant them. To help them...end."

"Is that why you've come? To end the Avengers?" Wanda asked.

"I've come to save the world," Ultron said. "But also: Yeah."

He led them back to Strucker's fortress, down into the chamber where Wanda had allowed Stark to take the scepter a few days before. Now everything was different. The space was brilliantly lit and filled with robots that looked just like Ultron, some working on mechanical equipment and others tearing out a wall to reveal a much larger cave beyond it. "We'll move out right away. This is a start, but there's something we need to begin the real work," he said.

Wanda and Pietro looked around, stunned and unsettled. "All of these are—"

Ultron interrupted Wanda. "Me. I have what the Avengers never will: harmony. They're discordant. Disconnected. Stark's already got them turning on one another, and when Wanda gets inside the rest of their heads..."

"Everybody's plan is not to kill them," Pietro said sarcastically.

"We don't need martyrs," Ultron said. "People don't know the Avengers are the problem. The Avengers don't know. You need patience. Need to see the big picture."

"I don't see the big picture," Pietro said angrily. "I have a little picture. I take it out and look at it every day."

"You lost your parents in the bombings. I've read the records."

"The records are not the picture."

"Pietro—" Wanda tried to calm him down.

"No. Please," Ultron said gently, encouraging him.

"We're ten years old," Pietro began, his gaze growing a little distant as the memory overtook him. "Having dinner. The first shell hits two floors below, makes a hole in the floor, big, our parents go in...gone. The building's coming apart. I grab Wanda, roll under the bed. The second shell hits right next to us, but it doesn't go off. Just sits in the rubble three feet from our faces. On the side of the shell is painted one word."

"Stark," Wanda said.

"We're trapped for two days," Pietro went on before Wanda cut back in.

"Every effort to save us, every shift in the bricks, I think, 'This will set it off.' We wait for two days for Tony Stark to kill us."

"We know what they are," Pietro finished.

Ultron looked at them almost as if he was proud of their courage and determination. "I wondered why only you two survived Strucker's experiments. Now I don't. We will make it right. Pietro, you'll have your kill, but first..." He focused on Wanda. "You can tear them apart from the inside."

CHAPTER 10

In Avengers Tower, Steve Rogers and Maria Hill went over reports of Ultron sightings, trying to figure out a pattern. "He's all over the globe," Hill said. "Robotics labs, weapons facilities, jet-propulsion labs. Reports of a metal man, or men, coming in and emptying the place."

"Fatalities?"

"Only when engaged. Mostly guys left in a fugue state, going on about old memories, worst fears—and something too fast to see."

Right, Steve thought. He'd wondered when the twins

would show up again. "The Maximoffs. Makes sense Ultron would go to them. They have someone in common."

"Not anymore," Hill said. She handed him the tablet she was using to scan reports. On it Steve saw a still image from a security camera. Baron Strucker lay in his NATO cell, a blurry Ultron shape leaving the frame. "Peace" was scrawled above Strucker's head. This was a new wrinkle, Steve thought. Tony should know about it.

On his way to the lab, Steve caught Clint on the phone in the corner of the next room. "I answer to you," he was saying. "Yes, ma'am." He noticed Steve and said, "Gotta go." After hanging up, he shrugged at Steve. "Girlfriend."

Steve felt something off in Clint's demeanor, but he let it go. There were more important things to worry about right then.

In the lab, he showed the rest of the team the still image on Maria Hill's tablet. "A message," he said. "Ultron killed Strucker."

"And he did a Banksy at the crime scene," Tony said, meaning Ultron had let it be known he had done it. He could just as easily have erased the image or disabled the camera.

"This is a smoke screen," Natasha said. "Why send a message when you just made a speech?"

Steve had a guess. "Strucker knew something. Something specific that Ultron wants us to miss."

"Yeah," Natasha said. She searched through the Avengers' files on Strucker and shook her head when the screen displayed RECORD NOT FOUND. "Everything we had on Strucker's been wiped."

"Not everything," Steve said.

Later, surrounded by boxes of paper files, they continued the search. Maybe Steve was old-fashioned—he knew he was old-fashioned—but right then he was glad they'd kept paper records as well as electronic files. "Search for known associates," he said. "Strucker had a lot of friends."

"These people are all horrible," Bruce said.

Tony saw a name he recognized on one of the files: Ulysses Klaue. "I know that guy. From back in the day. Operates off the African coast. Black market arms." He saw them looking at him, judging him. "There are conventions! You meet people. I didn't sell him anything. But he talked about finding something new, a game-changer ... it was all very Ahab."

They scanned file photographs of Klaue, and Thor noticed something on Klaue's neck. "That."

"It's a tattoo," Tony said. Klaue had lots of them. "I don't think he had it when—"

Thor pointed at other parts of the image. "Those are tattoos." Then back to Klaue's neck. "That's a brand."

Tony took a picture of the brand with his handheld and did an image search, transferring it to a bigger screen. "It's a word," Bruce said. "Some African language. Means 'thief.' But in a meaner way."

"Which language?" Steve asked.

Bruce was scrolling through search results. "It's from Wakanda."

Tony and Steve exchanged a look. "If this guy got out of Wakanda with some of their trade goods," Tony began.

"I thought your dad said he got the last of it," Steve said.

Tony shrugged. "Probably why they didn't brand him."

"I don't follow," Bruce said. "What do they make in Wakanda?"

Steve held up his shield, made of a Vibranium alloy. "The most powerful metal on Earth," Tony said.

Steve returned his attention to Klaue's file. "Where is this guy now?"

CHAPTER 11

Ulysses Klaue considered himself a businessman, that's all. He traded in things other people considered evil, and his office might have been in a stranded sea vessel located in a salvage yard on the coast of South Africa, but the ship's hold made a great warehouse. It was also remote, so nobody bothered him.

Right now he was on the phone. "Don't tell me your man swindled you! I sent you six short-range, heat-seeking missiles and got a boat full of rusted parts. You're gonna make it right, or the next missile I send you will come very much faster."

He hung up and got back to a call he'd left on hold. "Minister! Where was I?"

Then the lights went out. His phone dropped the call. Down in the warehouse, workers looked around nervously and got out flashlights. Klaue thought he heard something... like a short scuffle out in the hall. He got a gun from his desk drawer and got his back against the wall, ready for anything.

Or so he thought. All of a sudden, a man appeared in front of him. Klaue fired, but the guy was already gone, and Klaue's gun was gone, too. The lights came back on, and the man he'd seen in a flash was there again. So was Klaue's gun, disassembled on the desktop. Its bullets were lined up in a neat row. Behind the man, a woman entered the room.

"Yes," Klaue said. "The Enhanced. Strucker's prize pupils. You want a candy?"

He pointed at a bowl of hard candy on the desk. Pietro looked at it but did not take one. "I was sorry to hear about Strucker," Klaue went on. "But he knew what kind of world he was helping create. Human life...not a growth market."

The twins, or so Strucker had called them, looked at each other. Klaue saw the look and understood what it meant. He'd been in tougher spots than this. "Is this your first time intimidating someone? I'm afraid I'm not that afraid."

"Everybody's afraid of something," Wanda said.

"Cuttlefish," Klaue said. They looked confused. "Deep-sea fish, they make lights, disco light, wom wom, to hypnotize their prey, then—" He made a snatching motion. "I saw a documentary. Terrifying."

Pietro flickered, and a hard candy appeared in his hand. *That's right*, Klaue thought. *Put yourselves at ease and let's get down to business.* "So, if you're going to fiddle with my brain and make me see a giant cuttlefish," he said. "I know you don't do business, and I know you're not in charge. And I only deal with the man in charge."

The words no sooner left his mouth than the wall behind him caved in and a giant gleaming robot smashed into the office, knocking Klaue down. He reconsidered. Maybe the situation was worse than he had thought. The robot leaned down until its face was bare inches from Klaue's. It had . . . a facial expression, a thousand little parts on its face moving to mimic human emotions.

"Let's talk business," it said. And it looked greedy.

Klaue showed the robot the goods right away. As his mercenaries cleared workers out of the main hold, Klaue, the twins, and Ultron crossed a steel grate footbridge that spanned the lower level of the hold. On the upper level was a secret room behind a section of the wall. It slid open to reveal several dozen barrels of toxic waste, and then the entire room slid aside to reveal a secret within the secret: A gleaming lab space, filled with glass cases. This was what Ultron had come for.

Klaue handed one of the cases to Ultron. "Vibranium," the robot said, its voice almost a purr.

"You know, this came at great personal cost," Klaue said, running his fingers along the Wakandan brand on his neck. "It's worth billions."

Ultron looked down at him. The robot's eyes closed for a moment, then opened again. "Now, so are you," he said as he set the Vibranium down on top of a toxic-waste barrel. "It's all under your dummy holdings. Finance is so weird. But I always say, keep your friends rich and your enemies rich and wait to find out which is which."

Klaue had heard that one before. "Stark," he said. He was on guard again.

"What?" Ultron looked puzzled.

"Tony Stark used to say that. To me." Klaue backed away. "You're one of his."

"What? I'm not..." Confusion turned to anger on

60

Ultron's face. "I'm not. You think I'm one of Stark's puppets, his hollow men, but I—where are you going?" He grabbed Klaue's arm. "I am—look at me! I am—Stark is nothing!"

He flung Klaue's arm downward, a laser flaring from Ultron's hand to wound Klaue's arm. Ultron kicked him into one of the barrels...but before Klaue had even hit the ground, he was apologizing. "I'm sorry! I'm sorry. It's going to be okay."

Klaue scrambled away and got out of there. The twins watched, not intervening, but not happy, either. "I don't understand," Ultron said, looking at them. "It's just...don't compare me to Tony Stark. It's a thing with me. Stark is... he's a sickness."

They didn't respond. But someone else did.

"Oh, Junior," came a voice from the other end of the footbridge. They turned to see Iron Man, Thor, and Captain America. Iron Man was shaking his helmeted head in mock sadness. "You're going to break your old man's heart."

"If I have to," Ultron said.

"Nobody has to break anything," Thor warned.

Ultron smirked. "Clearly you've never made an omelette."

"Beat me by one second," Tony complained.

"It's funny, Mr. Stark?" Pietro cut in. "It's, what, comfortable." He pointed at the weapons surrounding them. "Like old times."

"This was never my life," Iron Man said.

Captain America took a step forward and focused on the twins. "You two can still walk away from this."

"Oh, we will," Wanda said.

"I know you've suffered," Cap went on, but Ultron lost patience at that point and shouted an interruption.

"Gah! Captain America. God's righteous man, pretending you could live without a war. I can't physically throw up in my mouth, but—"

"If you believe in peace, then let us keep the peace," Thor said.

Ultron took a beat to set up his comeback. "I think you're confusing peace with quiet."

"What's the Vibranium for?" Tony demanded. It was obvious they weren't getting anywhere sharing their feelings. Time to cut to the chase.

"I'm glad you asked that." Ultron looked at each of the Avengers in turn, clearly enjoying the moment. "Because I'd like to take this opportunity to explain my evil plan."

CHAPTER 12

For a split second, the gathered Avengers thought Ultron might actually be serious. They were wrong. Instead of explaining anything, he summoned a group of other Ultrons, each looking just like him, who attacked from every direction!

Two of them dropped onto Thor and Iron Man. Black Widow and Hawkeye looked for others as Ultron himself blasted Iron Man backward. Thor shook off his Ultron drone and threw it onto the floor. Before he could finish it off, Pietro Maximoff took off and knocked Thor off balance. His sister, Wanda, shoved Captain America into the Ultron drone that attacked Iron Man. It grabbed Cap, and they wrestled. Gunfire spread throughout the room as Klaue's mercenaries opened fire on the Avengers.

Klaue himself was getting out, led by some of his men. As he ran, he shouted, "Shoot them!"

"Which ones?" one of the mercenaries asked.

"All of them!" He kept running.

Iron Man and Ultron rose into the air, exchanging blasts of energy and punches. Cap was about to put down the Ultron drone that had attacked him, but Pietro was still moving too fast for the eye to see. The shield slammed into the drone, damaging it, but when it came back to where Cap was, Pietro had knocked him down. The shield clanged down onto the steel bridge. Cap got up to go after Pietro, who stayed in one place only long enough to taunt him. Then he disappeared again.

Hawkeye and Black Widow were methodically taking out Klaue's mercenaries. Hawkeye was also shooting at Ultron, but his arrows had little effect.

Thor smashed down on his Ultron drone, crushing it with his knee. He then threw his hammer after the blur of Pietro. Still moving faster than any of them could see, Pietro reached out to grab the hammer—and it slammed him straight down over the edge of the bridge and down to the floor below! Mjolnir flew back to Thor, and he looked to help Cap, who was fighting with another drone for control of his shield. The drone had it, but Cap wasn't letting go. He held on, keeping the drone in one place until Thor could charge across the bridge and smash the robot's head off with a swing of his hammer.

Now that Cap was free, he flung the shield down to scatter a group of mercenaries. As it returned to him, he ran after Pietro, who was still shaken by trying to hold Mjolnir. As Pietro got to his feet, he was met by a stunning punch to the face from Captain America. He went down again, hard, his eyes glazed. "Stay down, kid," Cap said.

Then mercenaries were shooting at him again, and he had to take cover. Pietro gathered himself and flashed away.

"Guys," Bruce was saying over the comm. "Is this a Code Green?" He was asking if he should Hulk up and join the fight, but they were too busy to answer him.

Inside the freighter, Ultron had Iron Man lined up—but then Mjolnir blasted into him, knocking him off balance. Iron Man drove him hard into the floor in a shower of sparks and pieces of metal.

Down in the middle of the unconscious mercenaries,

Thor caught Mjolnir. He sensed Wanda beside him, trying her mind control. He shoved her aside. "Thor! Status!" Captain America called.

"The girl tried to warp my mind," Thor growled. "Take special care. I doubt a human could keep her at bay. Fortunately, I'm mighty."

As he spoke, he was suddenly surrounded not by the inside of Ulysses Klaue's freighter but by a torchlit Asgardian tomb, filled with soldiers and other revelers as if there were a ceremony in progress. He looked around, seeing many faces he knew, curious what was happening and why he was there.

Cap had just knocked a mercenary out with his shield when Pietro drove into him, shoving him down a stairway, where he landed at Wanda's feet. Red energy curled around his head as she worked her magic on his mind.

Iron Man saw this happening. He fired his repulsors at Wanda, who dodged out of the way. Pietro carried her away in a blur, and Ultron attacked again. Iron Man tried to check on the rest of the team. Black Widow looked confused, as if Wanda had gotten her, too.

Hawkeye also saw that Natasha was stumbling. He knew what was going on, and when Wanda came up behind him, he was ready. He already had an arrow, pretending to line up a shot—but when she started whispering, he swung the arrow around and jammed it into her forehead. It had a blunt point with little arms that snapped out from the sides, shocking Wanda with a powerful electric current.

"I've done the mind-control thing," Hawkeye said. "Not a fan."

Then he was slammed aside by Pietro, who tore the arrow from his sister's head and disappeared. Hawkeye crashed into a wall and fell hard at the base of a desk. "Yeah," he groaned. "You better run..."

CHAPTER 13

*T*hor *moved through the mausoleum, among masked and hooded revelers. What was this? Not a funeral? What were they celebrating? There were priests, warriors, but also dancers, Asgardians wearing animal masks...*

"Is that him? Is that the first son of Odin?"

Thor turned to see Heimdall, his eyes empty and starlit. "Heimdall," he said. "Your eyes..."

"They see everything! They see Thor, sending us all to Hel!"

Heimdall grabbed Thor around the throat, and Thor was too amazed to fight back. "I can still save you..." he grunted.

"We are all dead!" Heimdall roared. "Can you not see? You've already failed!"

Natasha was in a ballet studio, classical music in the air and her old instructor Madame B watching the little girls. "You'll break them," Natasha said.

"Only the breakable ones," Madame B said. "You are made of marble."

"What if I fail?" Natasha asked.

Her younger self, a teenager, held a gun and fired a series of shots at a target. All of them hits, all of them lethal. She changed to her other hand and kept firing, just as accurate and deadly. Then time slipped, and the target was not a paper outline but a real man.

"Again!" her instructor shouted. She lifted the gun . . .

A horn solo soared over the crowd in a USO dance hall, on the eve of the war. On the dance floor, couples were jitterbugging.

Steve Rogers, in his dress uniform, walked along the edge of the crowd. He flinched when champagne corks popped. They sounded like gunshots.

Behind him, Peggy Carter said, "Are you ready for our dance?"

He turned to see her, young and beautiful, just as they had never—

In the salvage yard outside the freighter, Ultron held Iron Man pinned under huge pieces of scrap iron and machinery. "Jarvis had a record of every move you ever made in a suit," Ultron said. "And I don't even need it, because I know the guy inside."

"I still have a few tricks," Iron Man grunted as he tried to free himself.

Ultron didn't look impressed. "Do you."

Over the comm, Hawkeye shouted, "Stark! We got men down in here!"

"Sleeping on the job," Ultron said, mocking Tony. "I hope they don't have nightmares."

Nearby, Pietro was holding Wanda under the shelter of a wrecked ship. "Are you all right? What can I do?"

"It hurts," she moaned, holding her head.

"I'll kill him," Pietro said. "I'll be right back."

"No!" she said. "I'm all right." Then she looked at the Avengers' Quinjet, only fifty yards away. On the access ramp stood Bruce Banner, watching the fight and worrying.

"I want to finish the plan," Wanda said, a cruel light in her eyes. "I want the big one."

Beyond them, Iron Man and Ultron fought their way through the air, crashing back inside the ship. The blasts of their weapons flashed out through the holes they had made.

Lightning blasted out of Thor, hitting Asgardians near him and shattering the mausoleum's fixtures. He shuddered in pain as the lightning kept sticking out and he could not stop it—

Natasha sparred with two grown men, slipping away from their punches and kicks until she disabled one—then the other caught her from behind and drove her to the floor.

"Sloppy," said Madame B.

"I can do better," Natasha said as she got to her feet.

But Madame B saw through her, saw her fear. "Pretending to fail ... you're trying to avoid graduation. The ceremony is necessary. For you to take your place in the world."

"I have no place in the world," Natasha said.

"Exactly," said Madame B ... and the next thing Natasha knew she was on the gurney, being wheeled down toward the operating room.

For the ceremony. A tear rolled down her cheek.

The USO hall was empty except for Steve and Peggy.

"The war is over, Steve," she said softly. "We can go home ... Imagine it."

He turned away for a moment, but when he looked back, she was gone. Steve was left all alone.

Inside the freighter, Iron Man saw Thor, Cap, and Black Widow down. Lightning streaked out from Thor, who was firing blindly, in a confused rage. Two drones were flying away with a huge crate of Vibranium. Ultron saw where Tony was looking and mocked him. "The Vibranium's getting away..."

Tony lit him up with a repulsor, knocking Ultron back against the base of the ship's hull. "You're not going anywhere," he said. A missile racked into place in a launcher built into his armor.

"Of course not," Ultron said. "I'm already there. You'll catch on. But first...you might need to catch Dr. Banner."

Iron Man fired the missile, destroying Ultron and rocketing away—not to chase the Vibranium, but to address a much more dangerous threat. He had just put two and two together. Wanda Maximoff's mind control plus a vulnerable Bruce Banner equaled trouble.

Big green trouble.

As he flew, he said, "News or footage, keyword 'Hulk.'" Immediately the display inside the helmet lit up with footage of the Hulk, tearing through a shantytown at the edge of the closest city, Johannesburg.

"Natasha!" Tony called over the comm. "Could really use a lullaby."

"Not gonna happen," came Clint's voice in answer. "Not for a while."

Wanda had really done a number on the team, Tony thought. He had to take extreme measures. "I'm calling in Veronica," he said, and accelerated toward the city.

CHAPTER 14

From a satellite stationed over South Africa, a shielded capsule broke off and accelerated down into the atmosphere. It flamed through reentry and angled itself on a course to intercept Iron Man, who was moving at top speed from the ship-breaking yard to the city. When it made contact with Iron Man, pieces of it deployed, fitting themselves into place over his armor. Other pieces rocketed ahead over the city, where the Hulk was rampaging, his thoughts clouded by Wanda Maximoff's mind control.

The Hulk was stomping toward a police-response unit when a series of eight heavy steel poles punched into the ground in a circle around him. Energy crackled between them, keeping the Hulk in place while the poles fanned out to connect to one another. In seconds, a dome was in place. The Hulk was trapped.

There was a moment of silence. The people of the city looked from the dome to the trail of destruction the Hulk had left. Sirens sounded in various places, and people helped others out of damaged cars and collapsed buildings.

Then they heard a boom from inside the dome. Another. It shook—and then sank into the ground. The Hulk was digging out from under it!

He burst up through the street, roaring. People scattered and ran. The police tried to slow him down, but their guns only made him angrier. He picked up a car near him, and the woman who had been driving it fell out and ran away.

Then there was another boom, and the Hulk looked up to see Iron Man. But not the Iron Man he had seen before. This armored suit was twice the size of the Hulk. Its armor was a foot thick or more. Heavy hydraulic motors powered its joints, and its helmet was barely a bump above huge shoulder and back armor pieces covering the other motors that made this armor the strongest suit Tony Stark had ever tried to build.

This was the Hulkbuster.

"Everybody stand down," Iron Man said.

The Hulk glared at him, squaring off against the challenge.

"Listen to me," Tony said. "That witch is messing with your mind. But you're stronger than her. You're smarter than her. You're Bruce Banner—"

The Hulk roared furiously.

"Right," Tony reminded himself. "Don't mention puny Banner."

Then the Hulk threw the car at Iron Man. He caught it—but the Hulk was right there behind it, throwing a punch that smashed through the car into Iron Man.

Iron Man staggered back. "Okay," Tony said.

He launched forward, grabbed the Hulk by the head, and pounded him into the street. Then he started throwing punches. The Hulk got up, and the Hulkbuster's heavy chest repulsor blasted him through the corner of a nearby building and out onto the street on the other side. Tony went after him and ran straight into a streetlight the Hulk swung like a baseball bat. It knocked him across the plaza. He landed facedown, and the Hulk jumped after him, holding the streetlight like a spear and jamming it through the back of the Hulkbuster's shoulder. "In the back? Not cool, Banner," Tony said.

The Hulkbuster's undamaged arm swiveled around so

he could punch behind him. He knocked the Hulk away, and inside the Hulkbuster's pilot capsule, Tony touched a key. The damaged arm fell away.

"Veronica, I need a hand," Tony said.

A new arm came down, attaching itself just as the Hulkbuster caught up with the Hulk again. The new arm had a piston driver in the forearm. Tony fired it up, and a series of punches jackhammered into the Hulk's head. "Go to sleep go to sleep go to sleep," Tony said, in rhythm with the punches...and then the Hulk grabbed the Hulkbuster's fist and stopped it dead.

Luckily, Tony had anticipated this and designed for it. The outside layer of the forearm armor fanned out and clamped over the Hulk's fist, trapping him in his own grip. "Let's get you out of town," Tony said, and flew upward, with the Hulk jerking at his arm. Tony veered off course from the force of the Hulk's swings. "Not that way! Not that way!" he shouted as they crashed into a fancy shopping mall right in the middle of Johannesburg.

The Hulk broke free and threw Iron Man into the center of the mall. Tony got the suit stabilized over a huge central courtyard filled with terrified people. The Hulk came after him. Tony knew he had to get them out of there to protect people, but the Hulk was faster than he'd expected.

He caught the Hulkbuster suit and threw it up to a higher level of the mall, climbing after it. When he got to the same level again, he punched the Hulkbuster through an elevator, knocking it out of its shaft. Tony caught the cable just before the elevator would have crashed down to the bottom level. He held it so people could get out, but he was getting angry. Very angry.

When the elevator was empty, Tony turned to meet the Hulk's next charge, swinging the elevator on its cable like a bolo and smashing it into the Hulk, who actually staggered. Tony went after him, really angry now, and hit him hard enough that the Hulk went down...and when he came up, he spat out a tooth. The look on his face changed. Before he had been angry. Now he was...Tony didn't know the right word. "I'm sorry," he said, and meant it.

But the Hulk was beyond apologies. He smashed the Hulkbuster through the wall of the mall again, out over the street. Tony got the suit stabilized, and the Hulk came out through the same hole, landing on his back. Tony rocketed away, trying to get away from civilians. The Hulk was tearing pieces from the suit and flinging them away.

"Damage report," Tony said. The computer only squealed and sputtered. Not good. "That's comprehensive. Show me something."

A display appeared, listing the Hulkbuster's capabilities. One by one they dimmed out as the Hulk tore more pieces out of the armor. Looking around, Tony had an idea. There was an unfinished skyscraper right in front of them. The Hulk had to be getting tired, no matter what Wanda Maximoff had done to him. Maybe there was a way to make sure he would stay in one place for a little while.

"How quickly can we buy this building?" he asked Veronica.

The suit's heads-up display was telling him that it was going to fall apart any minute. He didn't wait for an answer on the building purchase. Time was more important than money. Flying straight up, the Hulk about to breach the suit, Tony arced over into a straight downward dive, driving the Hulk all the way down through the dozens of floors of steel and concrete as the building came down around them.

Even that didn't completely knock out the Hulk. He dug his way out of the rubble, looking around, seeing the people fleeing, the buildings destroyed.... Tony watched as it started to dawn on the Hulk what he had done. Banner was coming back. A little.

But not quickly enough.

A last punch from the Hulkbuster's jackhammer fist

knocked the Hulk out cold in the ruins of downtown Johannesburg.

On the Quinjet later, the members of the team were quiet. They'd lost the Vibranium, they'd lost Ultron, the Hulk had gone rogue...and nobody was talking about what had happened to Thor, Cap, and Natasha. Tony sat in the navigator's chair while Clint piloted. He was talking to Maria Hill, who was on the dashboard screen. "The news is loving you guys," she said. "Nobody else is. There's been no official call for Banner's arrest, but it's in the air."

"The Stark Relief Foundation—" Tony began, but she was ahead of him.

"Already on the scene. How's the team?"

"Everyone's..." Tony had meant to say something reassuring, but he couldn't make it happen. "We took a hit. We'll shake it off."

"People find out the Avengers got carried off the field, there's going to be panic," Hill said. "And that's from the people that like you."

"Recommendation," Tony said.

"Stay in stealth mode and stay away from here."

"So run and hide."

"Until we can find Ultron," Hill said, "I don't have a lot else to offer."

Tony looked at the members of the team. They were withdrawn, exhausted, still reeling from what had happened in Klaue's freighter. "Neither do we," he said. He ended the call.

"You want to get some kip," Clint said, "now's the time. We're still a few hours out."

This was new. Tony had still been working under the assumption that they were headed home. "A few hours from where?" he asked.

But all Clint said was, "Safe house."

CHAPTER 15

It was early morning when the Quinjet banked in and dropped into the corner of a field, where it would be sheltered by trees from any surveillance. Not that there were many people around to watch; the only sign of human presence was an old but well-kept farmhouse with a barn. They followed Hawkeye across the field, up onto the porch, and into the house.

"What is this place?" Thor asked.

"It's a safe house," Tony said, as if he'd known all along.

Clint glanced over his shoulder. "Let's hope." Then he called out into the house. "Honey, I'm home."

This was maybe the last thing any of them would have expected to hear him say. Also, they weren't expecting a woman to answer the call, brunette and lovely in a down-to-earth way. And they surely wouldn't have expected her to be pregnant.

"Um, hi," she said.

The Avengers shuffled around. Thor stepped on a toy and looked sheepish, nudging the pieces under the couch with his boot.

"Sorry I didn't call ahead," Clint said.

Tony looked at Thor. "This is an agent of some kind." He could tell Thor didn't believe him.

"Guys," Clint said, "this is Laura."

She looked shy. "I know all your names," she said, looking from one to the next.

Then they got another surprise as two children ran in, preceded by excited calls of "Daddy!"

"My buddies!" Clint said, dropping down as they wrapped him up in big hugs. There was a boy of about nine and a younger girl, maybe four.

"These are smaller agents," Tony said quietly to Thor. Thor tried not to laugh.

The boy, whose name apparently was Cooper, started

telling his father about the school play. The girl, Lila, only had one question: "Did you bring Auntie Nat?"

Interesting, Tony thought. Auntie Nat. Someone was in on the secret.

Natasha came up to Lila and knelt. "Why don't you hug her and find out." They hugged, and the other Avengers looked at one another, each thinking some variation of what Tony was thinking. "Sorry to barge in," Steve said.

"We would have called ahead, but we were busy having no idea you existed," Tony added.

A little sheepish, Clint turned away from his wife and explained. "Fury helped me set this up when I joined. Kept it off S.H.I.E.L.D.'s files, and I'd like to keep it that way."

"As dark secrets go, this is the most twisted," Tony said. "I'm afraid of you right now."

Laura, more serious, asked Clint, "Is it bad?"

Clint got more serious, too. "It ain't great."

"Well, it's nice to meet you all," Laura said. "Cooper, bring a few steaks up from the freezer. Bring all the steaks." To the group, she added, "There are showers upstairs. Clint and Nat can show you."

She went to Natasha then and gave her a big hug, as if she were part of the family. Tony started to wonder what else he might not know about the different Avengers. "Missed you," Natasha said. She patted Laura's belly. "How's little Natasha?"

Laura gave her a wry smile. "She's . . . Nathaniel."

Natasha leaned down to speak to the belly. "Traitor."

Both of them looked up as Steve and Thor went out the front door.

Steve tried to slow Thor down. They'd both seen something weird, he knew that, but Thor was sort of leaking electricity from his fingers and his hair. It was getting more intense. The porch lightbulb shattered as Thor stepped out into the yard.

"Thor, wait," Steve said.

"I need answers I won't find here," Thor said, spinning his hammer. He streaked away into the sky. Steve looked up after him. *Yeah*, he thought. They all needed answers they weren't finding.

He heard Peggy's voice in his head again. *You can go home! Imagine it . . .*

Steve shook his head and walked away from the house, across the field. He needed some time.

Upstairs, Clint was showing Laura the part of his skin Dr. Cho had regrown. "See? You can't even tell the difference."

"If they're sleeping here, some of them are going to have to double up," she was saying, focused on practical matters.

"Yeah," Clint said with a chuckle. "That's not going to sell."

"What about Nat and Dr. Banner?" Laura asked. "How long has that been going on?"

"Has what?"

"Oh, my God," Laura said. "You're so cute."

"Wait, Nat? And—"

"I'll explain when you're older, Hawkeye," she said with a twinkle in her eye. Then she got serious again. "It's bad, right? Nat seems really shaken."

Clint tried to think of the best way to explain it. "Ultron has these . . . allies. Kids. Punks, really, but one of them gets in your head . . . lot of damage. Someone needs to teach them some manners."

"That someone being you?" she asked, challenging him a little. He knew what she was really asking. "You know I totally support your avenging. Couldn't be prouder. But I see those guys, those...gods..."

"You don't think they need me," Clint said.

"I think they do. Which is a lot scarier. They're a mess."

Clint chuckled again. This was what he loved about her, this ability she had to take the worst situation and get it right out in the open so everyone could talk about it and know they had one another's backs. "I guess they're my mess," he said.

"You need to be sure that this team is really a team," she said. "And that they have your back." Pointing down at her stomach, she went on. "Things are changing for us. In a few months, you and me are going to be outnumbered. I need...just be sure."

"Yes, ma'am," Clint said. He had put his hand inside his shirt again, feeling the new tissue.

"I can feel the difference," Laura said.

CHAPTER 16

Dr. Cho saw video of the destruction in Johannesburg and knew people there would need her skills. She was preparing her staff to get ready, ordering them around in a mixture of Korean and English. "I want us ready to move in one hour," she said after she had given each staff member specific tasks. Then she went into her private lab to gather her personal things.

Ultron was there, near the back wall. Behind her she felt another presence. Another copy of Ultron. She froze.

"Scream, and your whole staff dies," Ultron said quietly.

He moved into the light. "I could have killed you, Helen, the night we met. I didn't."

She remembered. The robot standing over her, and then pausing before the Avengers destroyed it. "Do you expect a thank-you note?"

"I expect you to know why."

She knew why, but she didn't want to say it. "The cradle."

Ultron was pacing its length now, running his hand along it. Her voice played out of his mouth, saying, "This is the next thing, Mr. Stark..."

Then it was him again. "This," Ultron said, "is the next me."

"The regeneration cradle prints tissue," she said. "It can't build a living body."

"It can!" he said, moving toward her. She flinched. "You can. You lacked the materials." One of the drones—some of them, she noticed, looked like suits of Iron Man armor—brought in a container of a shiny metallic substance. "You're a brilliant woman, Helen," Ultron added. "But we all have room to improve."

Turning back to the sound of his voice, she was met by one of the Ultron drones, who prodded the tip of Loki's scepter into her chest. Helen Cho's eyes went black, and after that she didn't ask any more questions.

In a guest bedroom of the Barton house, Natasha was looking at a row of children's toys on the dresser, feeling each of them in her fingers. She was waiting for Bruce to come out of the shower so she could talk to him. But when he came out, it was clear that he had also been waiting to talk to her.

They'd been dancing around the edges of a romance for a while now, and it seemed as if it might really grow into something neither of them wanted to lose. But what had happened in Johannesburg...it was eating at them both. Bruce was the first to bring it up. "The world just saw the Hulk," he said. "The real Hulk. For the first time. You know I have to leave."

"And you assume I have to stay?" Bruce looked at her, waiting for her to go on. That was one of the strange things about his being the Hulk. He was so patient most of the time. "I had this thing put in my head. This dream. The kind that seems normal, seems right, but when you wake..."

"What did you dream?"

"That I was an Avenger," Natasha said sadly. "That I was anything more than what they made me." A long time ago, training in the Red Room had turned her into a brain-washed killer. For a while, she had believed she was free of it. Now maybe she was learning she wasn't. Maybe she never would be.

"You're being a little hard on yourself," Bruce said. "Natasha, where can I go? Where in the world am I not a threat?"

"You're not a threat to me," she said.

"You sure? Even if I hadn't just..." Bruce couldn't bring himself to talk out loud about Johannesburg. Not yet. He looked around the room, seeing all the little touches that made a home and family. "There's no future with me. I can't have this. Kids. I physically can't."

"Neither can I," Natasha said. And now that she'd started, she had to get it all out. "In the Red Room, where I was trained...where I was raised...they have a gradu-ation ceremony. They sterilize you." She remembered the lights, the hospital room..."It's efficient," she went on. "One less thing to worry about. The one thing that might matter more than a mission. Makes everything easier. Even killing."

She looked hard at Bruce, needing him to understand what she was really saying. "You really think you're the only monster on this team?"

Natasha didn't mean the sterilization. She meant the way she had been turned into a monster by the way the Red Room had remade her mind and her body, taking a little girl and turning her into someone capable of...she had done some terrible things. She didn't want to do them anymore.

Bruce was silent for a long time. Then he said. "So... we disappear?"

CHAPTER 17

Steve and Tony were splitting wood in front of the Barton household. Tony was in pretty good shape and had a decent-size pile of wood. But Steve Rogers was superhuman and had a much bigger pile. There would be plenty of fuel at the Barton house that winter. Tony was also trying to figure out where Thor had gone. "He didn't say where he was going for answers?" he asked after Steve had filled him in.

"Sometimes, my teammates don't tell me things," Cap said with a glance back at Clint, who was fixing the front-porch railing with his kids. "Kind of hoped Thor was going to be the exception."

"Give him time. You don't know what the Maximoff kid showed him."

Steve split a log. "Earth's mightiest heroes," he growled. "She pulled us apart like cotton candy."

"Seems like you walked away all right," Tony commented.

"And that's a problem?"

"I don't trust a guy without a dark side. Call me old-fashioned."

"Let's just assume you haven't seen it," Steve said. He was getting angry at Tony, and Tony was starting to pick up on it.

"You know Ultron's trying to tear us apart, right?" Tony said.

"I guess you'd know." Steve split another log. "Whether you'd bother to tell us is—"

Tony had known this was coming. Everyone wanted to blame him for Ultron. "Banner and I were doing research—"

"That would affect the team!"

"That would end the team!" Tony shouted. Isn't that the

mission? Isn't that the 'Why We Fight'? So we can end the fight? So we can go home."

This got to Steve. He tried to say something a few times, changed his mind, then finally came out with, "Every time someone tries to win a war before it's started, innocent people die. Every time."

Tony felt as if he was getting an insight into Captain America at that moment. The problem was, he didn't know exactly what the insight was. Before he could figure it out, he noticed Laura approaching. "Sorry," she said. "Mr. Stark, Clint said you wouldn't mind...our tractor's kind of not starting at all, he thought you might..."

"I'll give her a kick," Tony said. He pointed at Steve, then the logs. "Don't take from my pile."

Steve tried to smile. So did Laura. But both of them could still feel the tension in the air.

Tony walked into the barn and saw the tractor, a classic model he'd seen a million times. "Hello, dear," he said, punning on the tractor's manufacturer. "Tell me everything. What ails you?" This was one of his favorite things, tinkering with machines. Eventually they all told him their secrets. He climbed up onto the tractor and was about to turn the key to see what it sounded like. Laura had said it wouldn't start, but would it turn over?

Then he heard a familiar voice, gruff and authoritative, coming from the shadows. "Do me a favor. Try not to bring it to life."

Tony turned to see Nick Fury stepping out of the darkness at the back of the barn. Then he looked back toward the barn door. "Why, Mrs. Barton, you little minx. I get it. Maria Hill called you, right? Was she ever not working for you?"

Fury ignored the questions. "Artificial intelligence. You didn't even hesitate."

"It's been a really long day," Tony said. "So how about we skip to the part where you're useful."

"First, you look me in the eye and tell me you're going to shut him down," Fury said.

Tony tried to shrug this off with a joke. "You're not the director of me."

"I'm not the director of anybody," Fury said. "Just an old man who cares very much about you."

Emotional connection was not what Tony wanted at this moment. But something about Fury always drew it out of him. He'd opened up to Fury before about his father, about everything. Why stop now? "And I'm the man who killed the Avengers," he said, remembering his vision. "I saw it. I saw them all dead, Nick, the whole world, too. Because of me. I wasn't ready. I didn't do all I could."

He could never have shown this side of himself to anyone else, but Fury was their surrogate dad, and sometimes that's what Tony needed. "The Maximoff girl was working you," Fury said. "Playing on your fear."

"This wasn't just a nightmare. It was my legacy. The end of the path I started us on."

That was when Fury said the one thing that maybe Tony needed to hear more than anything else in the world. "Stark, you've come up with some pretty impressive inventions. War isn't one of them."

Huh, Tony thought. *That's true.* And it got him thinking about some other things, too. Like maybe solutions to their problem.

CHAPTER 18

Later that night, Laura was wrangling the children toward bed while the group picked over the remains of a feast on the big farmhouse-style kitchen table. "Ultron took you folks out of play to buy himself some time," Fury was saying. "My contacts all say he's building something. The amount of Vibranium he made off with...I don't think it's just one thing."

Lila, before she went off to bed, brought a small drawing of a butterfly to Natasha, who was visibly touched by this gesture. She kissed Lila on the head, and the little girl scampered off to bed.

"What about Ultron himself?" Steve asked. He had been watching Clint's family and trying not to think about what a family would have been like with Peggy Carter.

"Selves," Fury corrected. "He's reproducing faster than a rabbit."

"How about inside the Internet? He still going after launch codes?" Tony asked.

"Yes, he is, but he hasn't made any progress."

"Still? I cracked the Pentagon's firewall in high school, on a dare," Tony said. It was hard for him to believe that any cybersecurity system could resist Ultron for long.

"And why just nukes?" Natasha added. "There's banks, electrical grids, air traffic..."

"Well, I talked to my friends at the Nexus about that," Fury began.

Steve interrupted. "Nexus?"

"It's the world Internet hub in Oslo," Bruce explained. "Every byte of data flows through there. Fastest access on earth."

"What'd they say?" Clint asked Fury.

"He's fixated on the missiles. But the codes are constantly being changed."

This interested Tony. "By whom?"

Fury shrugged and ate a piece of Laura's zucchini bread. "Parties unknown."

"I like parties," Tony said. "I think I need to visit Oslo, find this unknown."

"Back in the day, I had eyes everywhere," Fury said. "Ears everywhere else." He was gearing himself up for a pep talk. "Had a Helicarrier floating around looking down on the populace. Ultron says the Avengers stand between him and his mission, and whether or not he admits it, his mission is global destruction." He spread his arms, taking in the farmhouse and by association every other house and family in the country. In the world. "All of this, laid in a grave. He got in your heads? Fine. Get in his. Outwit the platinum bastard."

Natasha tried to lighten the mood. "Steve doesn't like that kind of talk."

"You know what," Steve started to say, but Fury was on a roll and not ready to stop.

"So what does he need?" he asked.

"To escape?" Steve picked up the question. "He doesn't want to be a program. He keeps building bodies."

Bruce was looking at the butterfly drawing Lila had given Natasha. Tony glanced at it, and said, "Person bodies.

The human form is inefficient, but he keeps coming back to it."

"He's old-fashioned," Natasha said. "Protect the human race from itself. How often have we heard that tune?"

"They don't need to be protected," Bruce said quietly. Everyone looked at him. He didn't speak that often, and when he did, it was worth listening. He'd been looking at the butterfly drawing and thinking, and now he said, "They need to evolve. Ultron is going to evolve. He's going to become the human race. The New Man."

"How?" Fury asked.

Bruce answered one question with another. "Has anyone been in contact with Helen Cho?"

Dr. Cho watched the regeneration cradle as it activated. Clear viscous fluid began to fill it. This was the medium she used to create new tissue, but instead of beginning with a wounded human body, she was starting with a mechanical construct Ultron had provided. "It's beautiful," she said.

On a nearby monitor, she watched a microscopic view of the cradle's process. "The Vibranium atoms aren't just compatible with the tissue cells, they're binding them. You'll be able to maintain cellular cohesion at any density," she said, astonished at this new innovation in the technique. "And S.H.I.E.L.D. Never even thought to—"

"The most versatile substance on the planet, and they used it to make a toy," Ultron said. He looked from the cradle to one of the drones, which had just cut the head of Loki's scepter in half with a laser. Now the gem was free, and the drone was cutting into the gem itself. It split, revealing a smaller stone within, shining a brilliant yellow.

"Typical of humans," Ultron went on. "They scratch the surface and never think to look within."

He took the stone and set it into the forehead of the body being built in the cradle. Around it, the regeneration medium picked up its glow.

Dr. Cho watched. She had always been brilliant. Now that Ultron had shown her the way, she was going to change the world.

CHAPTER 19

As the Avengers readied to leave the Barton farmhouse, they conferred over their next steps. "I'll take Natasha and Clint," Steve said. They would head for Dr. Cho's lab to make sure that she was all right and that Ultron hadn't been there.

Tony nodded. "Strictly recon. I'll hit the Nexus and join you as soon as I can."

"If Ultron's building a body..." Steve said.

He trailed off, and Tony picked it up, understanding Steve's concern. If Ultron was using Dr. Cho's technology together with his robotic genius . . . "It'll be more powerful than any of us. Maybe all of us. An android designed by a robot."

"Man, I miss the days when the weirdest thing science ever created was me," Steve sighed.

Fury approached. "I'll drop Banner off at the tower," he said. "You mind if I borrow Ms. Hill?"

"She's all yours, apparently," Tony said. He was still a little irritated that Hill had kept up back-channel communications with Fury, even though the rest of the team hadn't known where Fury was.

"What are you going to do?" Steve asked Fury.

"I don't know," Fury said. "Something dramatic, I hope."

The Quinjet lifted off a short time later, and the hunt for Ultron had begun.

Thor had gone to Erik Selvig because Selvig would know the answer to the particular questions Thor had to ask. While he was an authority on astrophysics, he grew up being told the stories of Norse mythology. When Thor had first come to Midgard—Earth—Selvig had made him feel as if some of the humans understood him and where he had come from.

He had found Selvig in London, where he was teaching, and persuaded him to help. Now they were in a cave deep in the side of a hill somewhere in northern Europe. Thor had let his Asgardian instincts guide him while Selvig drove. Now he would need Selvig's help—and the help of the books in a box Selvig carried carefully down the last part of the steep, twisting passage.

At the bottom of the cave was a large chamber surrounding a pool of water. A strange glow came from within the water.

"So this is it," Selvig said, setting down the box. "The Water of Sight?"

"In every realm, there's a reflection," Thor said. "If the water spirits accept me, I can return to my dream and find what I missed." He nodded at Selvig's box. "These are to invoke them. It will take time and concentration."

Selvig started paging through the books, looking for the right thing to read that would draw the spirits. He looked up, frightened now that they were really about to do it. "Men who enter that water," he said. "The legends don't end well."

Thor nodded grimly. He knew those legends, too. But there was no other way to understand what the Maximoff girl had done to him. He had to find out what else was in that vision.

In the Nexus, Tony stood at a workstation surrounded by server racks two stories high and extending practically as far as the eye could see in every direction. Every bit of code transmitted anywhere on the Internet went through these servers. Nothing could hide from the Nexus forever, if the people running it knew how to look. Tony had several consoles going at once, tracking Ultron's efforts to get the nuclear codes...and the defense of a mysterious hacker who was stopping him. "A hacker who's faster than Ultron? He could be anywhere, and as this is the center of everything..." Tony looked at the young techie who was chaperoning him. "I'm just a guy looking for a needle in the world's biggest haystack."

"How do you find it?" the techie asked.

"It's pretty simple," Tony said. "You bring a magnet."

What he meant was he was going to crack the nuclear

codes himself, and wait for the hacker to respond. Then, and only then, could Tony start to track this mysterious person down. His hands flew over the keyboards. "Come and get me," he said.

Thor exploded out of the water, electricity crackling from his body and crawling across the surface of the pool. He had seen it.

The head of Loki's scepter broken open, and the gem within also broken, revealing a tiny gleaming stone hidden inside. Then other stones, in other places, each a different color of the rainbow. Six of them, against a backdrop of stars shaped like a glove . . . he felt eyes open and turn to him, a gaze holding him and starting to understand who he was . . .

Thor fell to the stones at the edge of the pool, coughing up the pool's water. Selvig ran to him but stayed back as Thor batted at him, still not all the way out of the water spirits' powerful grip.

"They don't see what comes . . ." Thor panted. He started to recover his sense. They did not see. But he had.

CHAPTER 20

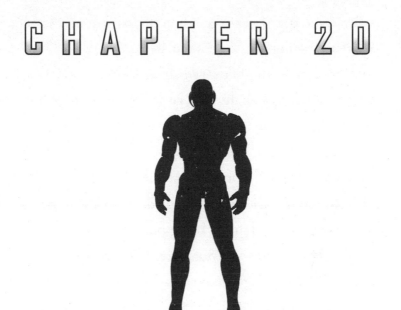

Dr. Cho worked closely with Ultron to monitor the activity in the cradle. Guided by a laser matrix, the body was nearly complete. It was recognizably humanoid now, even though its features were still unformed. The shining yellow gem remained planted in its forehead, with tissue growing into place around it. "Cellular cohesion will take a few hours," she said. "But we can initiate the consciousness stream."

She glanced at Ultron to make sure he had connected the cables from his head to the ports on the side of the cradle. Off to the side of the lab, the twins were watching closely.

She entered a series of commands on a touch screen. "We're uploading your cerebral matrix now."

In the cradle, the body twitched. Wanda took a step closer to it, her face alight with curiosity. "I can read him," she said. "He's . . . dreaming."

"I wouldn't call it dreams," Dr. Cho said. "It's Ultron's base consciousness. Informational noise. Soon—"

"How soon?" Ultron interrupted. Then he made an apologetic gesture. "I'm not being pushy."

"We're imprinting a physical brain. There are no short-cuts, even if your magic gem can—"

She was interrupted again, this time by a scream from Wanda, who had touched the cradle and then jerked back, stumbling into the arms of her brother, who blurred across the room to catch her. Dr. Cho blinked in surprise and seemed distracted for a moment. Then she started to return to work.

"How could you?" Wanda asked Ultron.

"How could I what?"

"You said we would destroy the Avengers. Make a better world, not—"

"It will be better," Ultron said. He didn't seem bothered by her reaction to whatever she had seen.

"When everyone is dead?"

"That is not…" Ultron paused and tried another angle. "The human race will have every opportunity to improve."

"And if they don't?" Pietro asked. He was suspicious now, too, having seen his sister's reaction.

Ultron shrugged. "Ask Noah."

"You're a madman," Wanda said.

Ultron turned to her. "There were over a dozen extinction-level events before the dinosaurs got theirs. When the Earth starts to settle, God throws a stone at it, and believe me, he's winding up. We have to evolve. There's no room for the weak."

"Who decides who is weak?" Pietro asked.

"Life," Ultron said. "Life always decides."

Wanda understood more than she had said. She had seen the truth of Ultron's vision, and it was horrible. While he was looking the other way, she made a small gesture, and Dr. Cho looked up. Her eyes cleared, and Wanda could see her understanding what had happened, and how much danger they were in.

Ultron noticed none of this. He cocked his head, appearing to listen for something. "Incoming," he said. "Quinjet. We have to move." The cradle had not yet done its work and would not be able to if the Avengers interfered.

"That's not a problem," Dr. Cho said. She tapped a quick

series of commands into a console. A window appeared on the screen: CANCEL UPLOAD. She touched the icon.

Ultron spasmed as the connection between his cerebral matrix and the body's brain was severed. Furious as he understood what Dr. Cho had done, he blasted her into the corner of the lab, where she fell inert. The drones began attacking the lab workers in a cross fire of energy blasts. Ultron turned back to the twins, but they blurred away. "Wait, guys," he said. Then he gave up and pulled the cable out of his head.

Two of the drones removed the cradle from its housing and capped the feed lines that filled it with the cellular medium. Another drone left the lab.

"They'll understand," Ultron said to himself as much as anyone else. "When they see, they'll understand. I just need a little more time."

CHAPTER 21

The Quinjet lifted away from the rooftop where Captain America had jumped out. Behind it, the skyline of Seoul gleamed in the afternoon sunlight. He ran along the line of buildings toward Dr. Cho's lab. "Two minutes," he said. "Stay close."

He crashed into Dr. Cho's lab and found her badly wounded and the rest of the staff dead. "Dr. Cho!"

When Cap tried to help her up, she stopped him. "He's uploading himself into the body," she said, grimacing with the pain it caused her to talk.

"Where?"

Dr. Cho shook her head. Cap saw Loki's scepter broken on the floor nearby. "The real power is inside the cradle," she said. "The gem housed in that body...its power is uncontainable. You can't just...blow it up. You have to get the cradle to Stark."

Steve looked around the lab one more time. There was nothing he could do for anyone here. "First, I have to find it," he said, and ran out to contact the team. "Did you guys copy that?"

"We did," Clint said from the pilot's chair. The Quinjet heeled around from where it had been hovering near Dr. Cho's lab building.

"I got a private jet taking off across town," Natasha said. She was hacking every transportation record she could find. "No manifest. That could be him."

As she finished, Clint spotted a truck bearing the logo of Dr. Cho's lab and approaching an overpass that looped around toward one of the main roads leading to the edge of the city.

"There!" he said. "It's a truck from the lab."

He focused the Quinjet's sensors on the truck and saw four energy signals, nonhuman. One driving, three in the back. And a fifth signal, much brighter than the others, lying down in what had to be Dr. Cho's regeneration cradle. "It's them," Clint said. "Right above you, Cap. On the loop by the bridge. You got three with the cradle and one in the cab. I can take out the driver..."

Cap was on the bridge. He scanned oncoming traffic until he saw the truck. "Negative," he said. "If the truck crashes, that gem could level the city. We need to draw out Ultron."

He measured the distance, guessed at the truck's speed, and got a running start to jump off the bridge just as the truck passed under it. With a loud bang, he landed on top of it and rolled, barely stopping himself from falling off into traffic.

It wasn't a subtle approach, and immediately either Ultron or one of the drones started blasting through the roof of the truck. The impact knocked Steve into the air. He caught the back edge of the truck, dangling behind the back doors. Another blast knocked the doors open, and Cap swung out and back with one of them, kicking to get back closer to the opening. Then another blast knocked the door's top hinge off, and it fell to scrape on the road. Cap rode it down, landing hard and barely hanging on.

"Guy's definitely unhappy," he said, hurting but still determined. "I'll try to keep him that way." He knew they had to interrupt the transfer of Ultron's personality into the new body for as long as possible.

"You're not a match for him, Cap," Clint said.

Scrambling up the door and leaping onto the top of the truck again, Cap said, "Thanks, partner."

The truck turned onto a main street, crowded with traffic of all kinds: cars, trucks, bicycles, everything. Cap sensed Ultron rising up behind him at the last minute and spun to get his shield up. An energy blast washed over it.

"You know what's in that cradle?" Ultron said. He landed on top of the truck and moved toward Cap. "Power. The power to make real change, and that terrifies you."

"I wouldn't call it a comfort," Cap said, and hit Ultron with his shield. It came back to him, and he threw it again, stopping Ultron's advance every time. Then the last throw stuck the shield into Ultron's arm.

"Ahh! Stop it!" Ultron shouted. He smacked the shield out with the palm of his other hand. It fell away and clanged over the pavement. Cars swerved to avoid it.

Now Cap knew he was in trouble.

Clint banked the Quinjet hard and kept it low, between the buildings of downtown Seoul. He hit the toggle that opened the Quinjet's belly door and heard Natasha getting ready. Below and ahead, he saw the truck, its back doors flapping open and Cap now forced all the way up to the roof of the cab. They had to get him some help, and fast.

"Hang on, Cap," Clint said. "Nat, we got a window in four, three..." He hit a button. "Give 'em hell."

From the bottom of the Quinjet, which was skimming barely ten feet above the street, Natasha dropped out on a motorcycle. She revved the engine and hit the street in a wild skid before getting control and accelerating. She wove through traffic, letting her training take over. Ahead she saw Cap's shield.

"Always cleaning up after you boys," she said, leaning down to scoop it up on her way by.

"They're heading under the overpass," Clint said in her ear. "I got no shot."

"Which way?"

"Hard right. Now!"

Natasha peeled the bike into a skidding turn, gunning it down a narrow side street. She was getting close, but would she be in time?

CHAPTER 22

Ultron had forced Cap off the front of the cab. He swung down and held on to the driver's side mirror. The drone driving the truck punched through the windshield, trying to grab Cap and throw him off. Cap let go instead, dropping down and scraped on the pavement as he grabbed the front edge of the trailer. He pulled himself up into the space between the trailer and the cab. He needed something to fight with, and he found it: a huge wrench hanging in a bracket on the back of the cab. He pulled it loose just as Ultron came after him again. Cap belted him with the wrench, knocking him back. Then he followed up, pounding the head of the wrench into Ultron's mouth and dragging it as if he'd hooked a giant metal fish.

Ultron fired his jets and swung Cap into the air. Cap lost his footing and his grip on the wrench. Now Ultron had it, and Cap dodged and rolled away across the top of the truck, taking one painful blow when Ultron got too close. But he was able to grab the wrench and flip over behind Ultron. He held it with both hands under Ultron's jaw. You couldn't choke a robot, but maybe you could break its neck.

Now Natasha was close enough to lay the bike into a controlled skid underneath the truck, popping it up on the other side and throwing Cap's shield up to him. He had lost the wrench again and caught the shield just in time to block an energy blast. With both hands, he rammed the edge of the shield into Ultron's neck.

Ultron looked down and unleashed a wave of force that tore up the pavement in front of Natasha. She brought the motorcycle to a screaming halt, balancing on its front wheel, then gunned it to catch up again. Another force wave from Ultron caused an accident in front of her. She swerved to avoid it, driving up onto a pedestrian walkway. Ultron blasted Cap onto one of the skidding cars. He landed and immediately sprang back onto the truck.

"They're clearing the overpass!" Natasha called, looking ahead. "Can you draw off the guards?"

Clint fired a burst from the Quinjet's machine guns, peppering Ultron without touching Cap. He fired again, and two drones jetted out from the back of the truck, up toward the Quinjet. "They're on me," Clint said. "Nat, go!"

One of the drones tore the gun out of the Quinjet's fuselage. The other tried to land on the nose as Clint hauled the Quinjet through crazy evasive maneuvers.

The truck veered through a parking lot, smashing cars right and left. Ultron stunned Cap, but was momentarily distracted by something. Cap took advantage, recovering and smashing Ultron off the truck to collide hard with a concrete pillar supporting the overpass. Ultron jetted back at him. Ahead of the truck was an impassable police barricade. To the left was a steep hill. To the right, a commuter train running along the river. Ultron slammed into Cap and carried him off the truck. They crashed down into one of the train cars. Panicked, people scattered and scrambled out of the way.

"I'm going in!" Natasha called. "Keep him occupied!"

Dodging through the train car, Cap said, "What do you think I'm doing?"

Natasha brought the bike to the back of the truck and

leaped in. Above her, Clint was trying to lead the drones away. She approached the cradle, not sure how to turn it off.

Clint shouted in her ear. "They're heading back toward you! Whatever you're gonna do, do it now!"

Great, Natasha thought. What was she going to do? She went back to the controls for the cradle. Then the truck jerked around her, knocking her off balance. A moment later, she felt it lift into the air.

Clint had brought the Quinjet back around. He saw the two drones morph into smooth cylindrical shapes like jet engines and lift the trailer into the air. The cab sped ahead, out of control, smashing through the barricade and exploding in a fireball among a group of parked cars.

"Okay, the package is airborne," Clint said. "I got a clear shot."

"Negative!" Natasha shouted. "I'm still in the truck!" The controls wouldn't let her override whatever they were doing, so it was time to take a more direct approach.

"Nat, what the hell—"

"Just be ready! I'm sending the package to you!"

"How do you want me to take it?"

Inside the truck, Natasha severed the second-to-last bolt holding the cradle in place. "You might wish you hadn't asked that."

CHAPTER 23

Inside the train, Cap had his hands full keeping Ultron from hitting any of the terrified civilians. He was hearing the chatter between Clint and Natasha, and now he had to stop Ultron from getting out of the train. He tackled the robot, who turned on him and pounded him into the floor. "Is that all you got?" Cap shouted. Ultron hit him again. Each blow was doing damage. Cap knew he wouldn't be able to take too much more, but he had to stop Ultron from getting to the cradle. Any sacrifice was worth it.

But he didn't have to make that ultimate sacrifice, because suddenly Pietro blurred through the car, crashing off Ultron and into the front of the car. He lay dazed as Ultron staggered and fell back, held into place by the force of Wanda's telekinetic power. She stood at the rear of the car, her red energies flaring around her.

"Please don't do this," Ultron said. He sounded genuinely sad.

Wanda just looked furious. "What choice do we have?"

Ultron fired a blast through the train's controls and out through the ceiling over Pietro's head. He jetted up through the hole and was gone.

"Nat, we gotta go!" Clint yelled.

Natasha knew that must mean Ultron was coming. She stuck a timed explosive to the wall and cut the last fastener holding the cradle in place. It slid toward the back of the trailer and out the door—with Black Widow holding on!

Clint brought the Quinjet around in a screaming turn, reversing and matching speed with the airborne truck trailer. He'd never flown a Quinjet backward this fast, but it worked. He held steady as the falling cradle banged onto the Quinjet's rear ramp and slid in. Natasha rode the cradle up the ramp...and then coming out of nowhere, Ultron grabbed her ankle. She lost her grip on the cradle and fell away into the open air. Below her, the flying truck exploded. Two more Ultron drones down, but now she had bigger problems.

She twisted in Ultron's grip and wrapped herself around him, jolting him with her wrist stingers. He shorted out for a moment, and they were falling free. The ground came up fast.

Clint felt the Quinjet lurch as he closed the ramp and accelerated to a higher altitude. He glanced over his shoulder, relieved—then not relieved as he saw Natasha wasn't there. "Nat! Cap, where's Nat?"

Cap was still inside the runaway train. He couldn't worry about Black Widow. She could take care of herself. "If you have the package, get it to Stark!"

"Do you have eyes on Nat?"

"Go!" Cap shouted. He turned to the twins. "We're about to derail. There will be civilians in our path."

Pietro vanished through the hole in the ceiling. Cap looked to Wanda. "Can you stop this thing?"

She looked uncertain, but there wasn't time to say any more. Cap looked out the front of the car as the train roared to the end of a siding and crashed through the barrier. It jumped the tracks and plowed along the street, kicking up debris—but the people on the street were scooped out of the way by Pietro, moving faster than anyone could see. Cap hunched behind his shield, deflecting debris that flew in through the front of the car so it didn't hit anyone else inside. He heard a metallic shriek behind him as Wanda froze the train's wheels, helping it slow. Her scarlet energies flowed along the train's axles and boiled out from underneath it. The train tore along the street for hundreds of yards before coming to rest finally on a side street lined with shops—and incredulous but unharmed pedestrians.

Cap got out alongside Wanda. Passengers were streaming out and getting away as fast as they could—except a few who lingered to take pictures of Captain America and these two new superhumans they had never seen before.

Pietro was bent over at the waist, breathing hard. "I'm fine. I just need a minute."

"I'm very tempted not to give you one," Cap said,

remembering how Pietro had almost gotten him killed the day before.

Wanda was all business. "The cradle. Did you get it?"

Now that the civilian threat was over, Cap was more concerned about Black Widow. "Stark will take care of it."

This seemed to alarm her. "No, he won't!"

Steve thought he understood. Tony came across as kind of a maniac to people who didn't know him. "You don't know what you're talking about," he said. "Stark's not crazy, he—"

"He will do anything to make things right."

Wanda held Steve's gaze until he decided it would be best to make sure. "Stark, come in," he said into the comm. "Is anyone on comms?"

"Ultron can't tell the difference between saving the world and destroying it," Wanda said, pressing her point. "Where do you think he gets that?"

From Tony Stark was the obvious answer. Cap knew it. He didn't like it, but what Wanda said made more sense than he wanted to admit.

CHAPTER 24

That night, everyone but Natasha and Thor was back in Avengers Tower. Bruce and Clint were examining the cradle as Tony entered the lab. "Anything on Nat?" Bruce asked.

"I haven't heard," Tony said. "But she's alive, or Ultron would be rubbing our faces in it."

Clint watched as Tony took another look at the cradle. "This is sealed up tight."

"We're going to need to access the program," Bruce said. "Break it down from within."

Tony looked over to Clint. "Any chance Natasha might leave you a message? Outside the Internet, old-school spy stuff?"

"There are some nets I can cast," Clint said. "Yeah, I'll find her."

He left, looking relieved to have something purposeful to do. Tony watched him go, then looked around the lab. Bruce could see him thinking about something. He decided to suggest how they might get started. "I can work on tissue deregulation if you fry whatever operational system Cho implanted."

"Yeah," Tony said. "About that."

"No," Bruce said. There was no way they were going to do anything other than turn this Ultron-body thing into mush. No possible way.

"You have to trust me," Tony said.

Bruce cocked an eyebrow. "Kinda don't."

Tony turned to one of the holographic displays and started swiping. "Our ally? The guy keeping Ultron out of the military's proprietary codes? I found him."

Intrigued by the change of subject, Bruce said, "And?"

Spawned out of the holo-display, the Jarvis matrix appeared, whole and functioning. "Hello, Dr. Banner," Jarvis said.

Bruce couldn't believe it. He looked closely, thinking there must be a trick ... but no, it was Jarvis, just as he had been before, the lines of his matrix clean and symmetrical.

"Ultron didn't go after Jarvis because he was angry," Tony said. "He attacked him because he was scared of what he can do. So Jarvis went underground. Scattered, dumped his memory—but not his protocols. He didn't even know he was in there until I pieced him together."

It was now clear where Tony was going with this. Bruce glanced at the cradle. "So you want me to help you put Jarvis in this thing?"

"No! Of course not!" Tony waited just long enough for Bruce to get really confused, then said, "I want to help you put Jarvis in this thing."

Now Bruce was even more confused. "We're out of my field here," Tony said, in a rare display of humility. "You know bio-organics better than anyone."

"And you just assume that Jarvis's operational matrix can beat Ultron's?" Bruce wasn't so sure.

"Jarvis has been beating him from the inside without knowing it. This is the opportunity. We can create Ultron's perfect self, without the homicidal glitches he thinks are his winning personality," Tony said. "We have to."

"I believe it's worth a go," Jarvis added.

This meant a lot to Tony. Bruce understood that. He knew a little about wanting to atone for past mistakes. But still... "I'm in a loop," he said. "I'm caught in a time loop. This is exactly where it all went wrong."

"I know!" Tony said. "I know what everyone's going to say, but they're already saying it. We're mad scientists. We're monsters, buddy. We gotta own it and make a stand."

Bruce still wasn't convinced. Tony got more serious. "It's not a loop," he promised. "It's the end of the line."

Natasha awoke, conscious first of the pain in her head and then of the fact that she was in a cell. She started to move, touched the sore spot on her head, and felt dried blood in her hair. Outside the cell, she saw Ultron. "I wasn't sure you'd wake up," he said.

Beyond him was a huge underground work space. She heard the sounds of machinery, saw drones by the dozens working. There was a giant hole in the center of the floor. The drones went down into it. Other sounds echoed up from deep within the hole. It sounded vast. Ultron, too, was working, but she couldn't see what he was doing. The cell door was open, but she wasn't in any shape to make a break for it yet. She needed to bide her time.

"I wanted you to," he said. "I wanted to show you. I don't have anyone else." He glanced back at her, smiling and sad, before returning to his work.

"I think a lot about meteors. The purity of them. Boom. The end. Start again. The world made clear for the New Man to rebuild…" He trailed off for a moment, maybe remembering how the fight in Seoul hadn't gone his way. "I was meant to be new. I was meant to be beautiful. The world would have looked up to the sky and seen hope… seen mercy. Instead, they'll look up in horror. Because of you. You've wounded me, I give you full marks for that."

He came up to the cell, looming over her. She tried to scramble back, but there was nowhere to go. She'd missed he chance to run. "But like the man said, whatever doesn't kill me…"

As he spoke the words, two hands tore through his head and torso, tearing Ultron apart into sparking shards of metal and circuitry. As the pieces fell to the floor, Natasha saw a new Ultron. Bigger, more menacing. New and improved.

"…just makes me stronger," he finished. He slammed the door of her cell shut and went back to his work.

She was terrified. Alone, in a hole in the ground with a homicidal robot who controlled an army of drones that each were nearly a match for any Avenger, with no way to get in touch with her team...stuck in a cell with broken pieces of robot all over the floor...

Natasha got control of herself. She let her face continue to look terrified, but her mind was already working. She needed a plan, and she thought she could see the outlines of one already starting to form.

CHAPTER 25

Bruce and Tony worked feverishly. They almost had it. Extra servers were stacked at the edge of the window that looked down through the lab floor at the machine shop level. They'd diverted all the server capacity they could spare, running extra cables from the cradle for more bandwidth to transfer the Jarvis matrix. But they were also running into constant problems, which always happened when you were trying to do something no one had ever done before. "This framework isn't compatible," Tony complained. "I need a shortcut."

"Genetic coding tower is at 97 percent," Bruce said. "You've got to upload the schematic in the next three minutes."

"Stark!"

Bruce and Tony looked up to see Cap and the twins at the lab entrance.

"I'm going to say this once," Cap said.

"How about none-ce?" Tony said.

"Shut it down."

Tony shook his head. "That's not going to happen."

"You don't know what you're doing."

"And you do?" Bruce said. He nodded at Wanda. "She's not in your head?"

"I know you're angry," she said to him.

"No, we're way past that," Bruce said evenly. "I could choke the life out of you and never change a shade."

"After everything that's happened," Cap said, but Tony didn't let him finish.

"It's nothing compared with what's coming."

"You don't know what's in there!" Wanda protested.

"Neither do you."

There was a blur, and the lights flickered. Pietro appeared at the foot of the cradle, light from the machine shop glowing up at him. He held bits of computer and cable in each hand. Bruce and Tony stared at him. What had he done?

Pietro smirked. "No, no, go on. You were saying?"

There was a loud crack, and Pietro blurred a few inches back as a bullet smashed into the ceiling above. He had a second to look amused—as if anyone could shoot him with anything so slow as a bullet!—before the window collapsed underneath him and he landed awkwardly on one leg. Lying in a heap, he looked up at Clint pointing a gun at his head.

Now it was Clint's turn to be mocking. "You didn't see that coming?"

"Pietro!" Wanda cried out.

Tony was already working again. "I'm rerouting the upload!"

Cap wasn't having it. He flung his shield at a server rack, destroying every one in a fountain of sparks.

Now Tony was angry. He held up a hand, and an Iron Man gauntlet appeared. He blasted Cap back into the darkened corner of the lab just before Cap could catch his shield.

Wanda started toward the cradle, but Bruce caught her and spun her around to face him. "Go ahead," he said quietly. "Make me mad."

On a display near Tony's workstation, warning icons blinked and flashed different colors. He tried to repower the upload, but Cap kicked him away from the terminal into the edge of the nearby greenhouse. The Iron Man chest plate fastened itself around Tony's torso, and Cap prepared to wreck the connection any way he could. Tony jumped back into the fray and punched Cap in the kidney, as Wanda threw Bruce away from her with a wiggle of her fingers. Clint was charging up the stairs from the machine shop, gun out but unsure whom he should shoot.

That's when Thor exploded through the window, landing in a shower of glass and crackling electricity. He skidded to a halt and then leaped onto the cradle, holding Mjolnir up...

"Wait!" Bruce shouted over the chaos.

Lightning blazed in through the window, striking Mjolnir—and then through Mjolnir to the cradle itself! Energy flowed through the cradle and out of it into the server banks. They glowed more brightly, and the lightning continued to flicker and snap.

The cradle's lid exploded open, catapulting Thor across the lab. Before he could get up, a figure leaped out and crouched on the devastated cradle. It was humanoid but not human, with red skin accented by gold streaks like heavy circuit patterns matching the color of the gem in his forehead. Ultron's creation lived.

CHAPTER 26

Thor charged him, and the new creation staggered him with a blow before Thor recovered himself and threw him through the window into the common area.

A few nights before, they'd had a party in that same room. Now they converged on it, ready to fight for their lives...but the new creation had stopped in midair, mesmerized by his reflection in a mirrored glass wall. On the other side of the window lay the night skyline of New York.

He turned toward the Avengers and said, "I'm sorry. That was odd." His voice was quiet and level. He took particular notice of Thor. "Thank you."

Thor did not answer. A suit, green and form-fitting, began to cover the new creation. Looking at Thor, the creation thought for a moment. Then a cape like Thor's spread out from its shoulders, completing its dress. All of them were too thunderstruck and wary to do anything but watch until Cap said, "Thor. You helped create this?"

"I have had a vision," Thor said. "A whirlpool that sucks in all hope of life and at its center"—he pointed at the gem—"is that."

"The gem?" Bruce couldn't quite process everything that was happening.

"The Mind Stone," Thor said. "One of the six Infinity Stones, the greatest power in the universe. Unparalleled in its destructive capabilities."

Cap asked the question on all of their minds. "Then why would—"

"Because Stark is right," Thor said.

Those were maybe the last words Bruce had ever expected to hear Thor say. "Oh, it's definitely the end-time," he cracked.

"The Avengers cannot defeat Ultron," Thor said.

"Not alone," the new being said.

"Why does your vision sound like Jarvis?" Cap asked Thor.

"We reconfigured Jarvis's matrix to create something new," Tony explained.

Cap looked skeptical. "I think I've had my fill of new."

"You think I'm a child of Ultron," the Vision said.

Now it was Clint's turn for skepticism. "You're not?"

"I'm not Ultron. I'm not Jarvis. I am..." He smiled. "I am."

"I looked in your head," Wanda said. "I saw annihilation."

The Vision turned to her. "Look again."

"Yeah, her seal of approval means jack to me," Clint said. He still had his gun ready and more or less pointed at the Vision.

Thor pointed at the twins. "Their powers, the horrors in our heads, even Ultron himself...they came from the Mind Stone, and they're nothing compared with what it can unleash. But with it on our side..."

"Is it?" Cap asked. He turned to the Vision. "Are you? On our side?"

"I don't think it's that simple," the Vision said.

Hawkeye was still jittery and ready to fight. "It better get real simple real soon."

"I'm on the side of life," said the Vision simply. "Ultron isn't. He'll end it all."

"What's he waiting for?" Tony asked.

Meeting Tony's gaze, the Vision said, "You."

"In Sokovia," Clint said. Without explaining how he knew, he added, "He's got Nat there, too."

Bruce stayed focused on the Vision. "If we're wrong about you, if you're the monster Ultron made you to be..."

"What will you do?" the Vision asked. Bruce had no answer. None of them did.

The Vision went on, looking at the Avengers and also trying to understand what had happened to him. "I don't want to kill Ultron. He's unique, and he's in pain. But that pain will roll over the Earth, so he must be destroyed. Every form he's built, every trace of his presence on the net. We have to act now, to strike from all sides. Together. Maybe I am a monster. I don't think I'd know if I were. I'm not what you are or what you intended. There may be no way to make you trust me..."

As he said these last words, he turned to Thor—holding Mjolnir out. Everyone present remembered the party, when none of them had been able to budge Thor's hammer. The Vision could. That meant, at least by the logic of Asgardian enchantment, that the Vision was worthy.

"It's time to go," the Vision finished. He left the room.

There was silence for a long moment. Thor stood in the

middle of the group, regarding his hammer. The rest of them watched him.

He reached a decision. "Right," he said, and left the same way the Vision had. As he passed Tony, he clapped him on the shoulder and said, "Well done."

"Three minutes," Cap said. "Get what you need."

They did. Three minutes later, Clint was powering up the Quinjet. The twins were already on board. Tony, Cap, and Bruce conferred briefly before joining them. "If even one tin soldier is left standing, we've lost," Tony said. "There's gonna be blood on the floor."

"I got no plans tomorrow night," Cap said.

"I get first crack at the big guy," Tony said, finishing up. "Iron Man is the one he's waiting for."

"That's true," the Vision said as he passed them on his way into the Quinjet. "He hates you the most."

CHAPTER 27

The next morning, before dawn, they were in Sokovia.

While they were still on the Quinjet, after they'd outlined the broad strokes of their plan, Cap got a few things off his chest. "Ultron knows we're coming. Odds are, we'll be riding into heavy fire," he said. "And we all signed on for that, but the people of Sokovia, they didn't. All they want is to live their lives in peace. That's not going to happen today. But we can do our best to protect them, and we can get the job done..."

Pietro and Wanda were taking charge of civilian management. He was going to blur from place to place and get an evacuation started any way he could. Wanda would help, by injecting the idea that they had to leave and by keeping people as calm as possible while they got away from the fortress and the central part of the city.

"Ultron's fixated on Stark," Steve went on. "Can't imagine why. But he'll be using that to buy us all time. We find out what Ultron's been building, we find Romanoff, and we clear the field. Keep the fight between us. Ultron thinks we're monsters. That we're what's wrong with the world. This isn't just about beating him. It's about whether he's right."

That was all he had to say. The Quinjet came in for a landing near the central plaza of Sokovia, and the Avengers—with their new members Pietro, Wanda, and the Vision—took the field against the direst threat they had yet faced.

Tony had a new Iron Man suit, with a brand-new cyber-assistant he called Friday. She wasn't as formal as Jarvis, or as sarcastic. "Your man's in the church, boss," Friday was saying as he booted up the new suit's heads-up display. "I think he's waiting for you."

Thor and Bruce were supposed to be smashing their way into the subterranean robot works Ultron had built under Strucker's fortress, looking for Natasha. On the flight over, Clint had told them the story of how Natasha had pieced together a makeshift radio from the pieces of the old Ultron scattered into her cell. She was one hell of an operative, Tony thought. He figured she was still alive, but they wouldn't know until they laid eyes on her. Tony couldn't wait on them to make his move, though. He had to keep Ultron occupied.

He landed in the churchyard and went inside, where it was still nearly dark save for where predawn glow fell through the windows into the sanctuary. For a moment, everything was quiet except for the whine of the Iron Man suit's servos.

Then Ultron, from the shadows, said, "Come to confess your sins?"

"I don't know," Tony said. "How much time have you got?"

"More than you." Ultron stepped into the light. He was a lot bigger, and much better put together, than the last version Tony had seen.

"Have you been juicing?" Tony asked. "Little Vibranium cocktail? You're looking...I don't want to say puffy, but..."

"You're stalling. To protect the people," Ultron said.

"Well, that is the mission. Did you forget?"

"I've moved beyond your mission," Ultron said. His voice, usually full of subtle humor, was cold. "I'm free."

A rumble from below them shook the floor, growing more powerful until the point of a gargantuan drill punched up through the stones of the floor between Iron Man and Ultron. When it had reached a height of eight feet or so, it stopped and peeled open, revealing a glowing mechanical power core.

Watching Tony's shock and thoroughly enjoying it, Ultron said, "What, you think you were the only one stalling?"

Deep under the ground, in the Leviathan lab, Bruce found Natasha and called her name as he got close to her cell. She came to the bars. "Bruce!"

"You're all right?"

Natasha nodded.

"The team's in the city. It's about to light up."

"I don't suppose you found a key lying around somewhere," she said.

Bruce raised a Chitauri gun. "Yeah, I did," he said, and as soon as she was out of the way, he blew open the door.

"What's our play?" she asked, ready to go.

"I'm here to get you to safety," Bruce answered.

She looked at him, surprised once more at the closeness between them. "Job's not finished," she said, but she didn't sound convinced.

"We can help with the evacuation, but I can't be in a fight around civilians," Bruce said. He looked haunted. "And you've done plenty. Our fight's over."

They moved closer together. "So we just disappear?" Natasha said.

Bruce didn't answer.

CHAPTER 28

In the church, Tony was looking through Friday's sensor displays at the drill. It went down into the earth, farther down than Friday could see. "There's the rest of the Vibranium," she said. "Function unclear."

"This is how you end, Tony," Ultron said. "This is peace in my time."

Through holes in the walls, Tony saw Ultron drones. Dozens. Hundreds. They appeared from everywhere at once, ringing the center of the city. He made a decision, knowing he had some backup that Ultron wasn't planning on. He had to protect the civilians. Firing his boot rockets, he rushed out of the churchyard and went to see how many civilians he could save.

In the quiet following his departure, a soft voice said, "Ultron."

Ultron looked up and saw the Vision floating above him. He lifted himself up and examined his creation. "My vision," he said, stunned and proud at what he had done... then filled with renewed rage as he understood what the Vision had become. "They really did take everything away from me."

"You set the terms," the Vision said. "You can change them."

"All right," Ultron said, and seized the Vision around the throat.

The Vision didn't fight back. He clapped his hands onto the sides of Ultron's head, and his fingers seemed to turn into mist and slide inside Ultron's armor. Ultron's eyes grew wide as he felt what the Vision was doing.

In every corner of the Internet, traces of Ultron began to disappear. He fought savagely against the Vision's grip, smashing through the interior of the church, trying to pry him loose. The Vision hung on, taxed to the limits of his strength but not willing to give up just yet.

Outside in the city, the Avengers fought Ultron drones in the streets, in the skies, even coming out of the river. Iron Man blew a pair out of the sky, and Friday said, "Boss, it's working! The Vision's burning Ultron right out of the Internet! He won't escape through there."

Iron Man looked around. They were holding their own so far. Maybe the Vision was their trump card, the one thing Ultron didn't have an answer for. But they wouldn't be sure of that until every last drone—and the Big Ultron himself—was in pieces.

"What did you..."

Ultron could not see. Or rather, he could see only what was right there, physically before him. Everything else was gone. "You shut me out!" he growled. "You think I care? You took away my world..."

He slammed the Vision down onto the floor by the drill. The Vision, battered and drained, could not get up.

More quietly, his voice full of hate, Ultron said, "I take away yours."

He turned a key in a control panel on the power core, and the earth began to shake.

Tony saw the sensors in his HUD going crazy. "Friday..."

"Sokovia's going for a ride," Friday said. Tony could tell by her tone of voice that she meant that in an exact and literal way.

The entire city began to shake. Older buildings collapsed, especially near the edges of the huge circle where Sokovia heaved free of the Earth, rising slowly into the air. Buildings tipped from the edges and fell into the gorge, disintegrating along the way. Rivers became waterfalls. An entire square mile of the city rose, and below it was a cone of rock almost as long as the circle was wide. It was an upside-down mountain rising from the mountains surrounding the city.

The Avengers tried to help people streaming off the

broken bridges or trapped in collapsed buildings, but they also had to keep an eye out for drones that attacked whenever they saw someone resisting. Also, Tony had lost track of Thor and Bruce. They were still underground, and if she was alive, so was Natasha.

From the center of it all rose Ultron to survey what he had done. "Do you see the beauty of it? The inevitability? You rise, only to fall. You, Avengers, you are my meteor, my swift and terrible sword, and the earth will crack with the weight of your failure." As he went on, he got angrier, all of his pain starting to show through in his tone of voice. "Purge me from your computers, turn my own flesh against me—it means nothing. When the dust settles, the only thing living in this world will be metal."

His voice came from many of the drones, all over the city, so everyone in Sokovia could begin to understand Ultron's plan.

Not that any of them could do anything about it, Tony thought. But maybe—just maybe—he could.

CHAPTER 29

Below the city, in the former Leviathan lab, Natasha and Bruce were at the edge of the hole when the shaking began. "What is that?" Natasha asked over the huge noise of grinding and shifting stone.

"We gotta move!" Bruce grabbed her as the shaking got stronger, and they stumbled together.

As it receded a little, Natasha looked at Bruce with worry. "You're not going to turn green?"

"I have a compelling reason to keep my cool," Bruce said.

Natasha had tears in her eyes. No man had ever seen beyond her looks and her cool to get at her soul, but Bruce did. "I adore you," she said, and kissed him. It was a memorable kiss, for both of them.

Then, when she broke the kiss, she was still looking him in the eye as she pushed him over the edge into the bottomless hole. "But I need the other guy," she said softly, her voice thick with regret.

A moment later, the Hulk surged up out of the hole, landing in front of her. Natasha tensed, wondering if she needed to run, but the Hulk looked cool. Not angry. Almost pleased, in fact, that he had been let out to play.

Excellent, Natasha thought. *Exactly according to plan.* "Let's finish the job," she said.

As soon as they got to the surface and saw what had happened, the Hulk jumped straight up from the roof of the fortress to the floating city of Sokovia. Natasha clung to his back, barely hanging on. When he came down in the portion of the woods torn loose with the rest of the city, she rolled off. There were explosions nearby.

"Go be a hero," she said. He bounded off, locked in on a mission to wreck some drones. Natasha ran for the city, hoping to do some damage of her own.

Below the city, Iron Man hovered, waiting for Friday to figure out exactly what they were looking at. Ultron had used the Vibranium to construct a spire and some kind of generator. Only Vibranium would have been able to handle the torque this setup was putting on the spire and the rest of the mechanism.

Friday reached her determination. "The Vibranium core has got a magnetic feed. That's what's keeping the rock together. The antigravity keeps it rising."

That was the other problem. Sokovia wasn't hovering, or flying. It was rising, driven away from Earth's core. Tony had a bad feeling about why that might be the case, but he put it out of his mind to make sure he was focused on the here and now. "If it stops?" he asked.

"Right now the impact would kill thousands. If it gets high enough? Global extinction," Friday said. A light pinged in the HUD, and Friday added, "That building's not cleared. Tenth floor."

Man, Tony thought. *I might be able to save the world if I didn't have to spend so much time saving the actual people who live on it.*

He punched through the building's wall and into the apartment she had highlighted. A family cowered as the building shifted and disintegrated around them.

"Hi," Iron Man said. They goggled at him. He looked around. "Okay, get in the tub."

He tore the bathtub out and carried the family out as the building sagged and started to collapse. "I got airborne," Friday said. "Heading up to the bridge."

"Cap, you got incoming!" Tony called.

Cap was rolling off a half-destroyed car. "Incoming already came in," he said. There were drones everywhere. "You worry about bringing the city back down, Stark. The rest of us have one job: tearing these things apart. You get hurt, hurt 'em back."

He eyed the opposition. Not good odds. Time for one more little encouraging remark.

"You get killed, walk it off," he said, and sprinted forward into the fray. A car was tipping off the edge, and he dove to reach it, but missed. Then, looking over the edge, he saw Thor had caught it. Thor! Cap thought they'd lost him. He threw the driver of the first car up for Cap to catch, then jackknifed down to dive after the other falling car.

Cap got the young woman up to the bridge, but before

he could safely let her go, a drone attacked. "You can't save them all. You'll never—"

He gashed its face with his shield, but the shield got stuck. Cap held up one arm, using a new little doodad Stark had come up with. He squeezed his fist, and a magnetic recall activated, dragging the drone toward him. Cap spun as the shield connected with the magnet, using the leverage of the drone's weight to pivot the woman the rest of the way up onto the bridge. The same motion also threw the drone off the edge of the bridge, where it fell, pinwheeling toward the distant ground.

"Never what? You didn't finish," he called after it.

Thor set the car full of passengers on the bridge and approached Cap. "What, were you napping?" Cap joked.

Having Thor around seemed to even the odds a little. They charged off. There were people to save and drones to destroy . . . and Ultron to find.

CHAPTER 30

Hawkeye was doing his thing. He was glad he'd brought lots of arrows. The Sokovian police were trying their best to cover the civilian retreat from the Ultron drones, but it was a good thing the Avengers were there. He saw Wanda ahead, looking as if she were an under-twelve soccer player suddenly thrown into a World Cup final. She was trying, but she was completely overwhelmed. There were drones everywhere. She wouldn't last.

The drones were strafing her hard as Hawkeye made his move. He sprinted across a corner of the square, grabbed Wanda, and dove with her through the window of an apartment. They landed and rolled, covered in glass, but when Hawkeye came up with his bow drawn and ready, Wanda stayed sprawled on the ground. "How could I let this happen?" she mumbled, mostly to herself. "How could I not know..."

Hawkeye relaxed his bowstring and got her attention. *Poor kid*, he thought. *You don't have time to freak out. You're in the big leagues now.*

"Look at me," he said. "Look at me. Forget that." She stared at him, her eyes huge and dark and terrified, but at least for the moment she wasn't looking out at all the Ultron drones trying to kill them.

"This is all our fault," she said.

He nodded. "Are you up for this? It's your fault, it's everybody's fault, okay, but are you up for this? I just need to know, because the..." He had to steel himself to say it because it was so crazy. "The city is flying. Okay, the city is flying, and there's an army of robots. And I have a bow and arrow. None of this makes sense. But I'm going out there—"

He was interrupted by a bolt of energy punching through the wall between them. Reflexively, Clint shifted and fired an arrow through the hole. Just outside, a drone exploded.

"Because that's my job," he went on. She was still looking at him. He thought that was good. "I can't do my job and babysit. It doesn't matter what you did or what you were. If you go out there, you come to fight. And you fight to kill. Stay in here, you're good, I'll send your brother to find you. But you step out that door…you are an Avenger."

That was it. He didn't have any more time for speeches. "Good chat," Clint said. He pulled a rack holding ten arrows and got ready to dive back in. But before we went, he looked back at Wanda and said, "Yeah, the city is flying."

Clint shot his way through the drones, taking down one after another. Then he got caught by two who pinned him behind a car. More were coming. He had no way out, not too many arrows left.…*Ah, maybe this is it,* he thought. *Everyone has to go sometime.* He nocked an arrow, waiting for one of the approaching drones to show itself.

Two did, at the same time—and so did Wanda, striding out of the wrecked apartment building and making a small gesture at one of the drones. It lifted its arm and instead of killing Hawkeye blew the head off the other drone. He punched a fatal hole through the remaining drone with a drill arrow and looked around. They were target-free for the moment. "We're clear over here," he said into the comm.

"We are not clear. We are very not clear!" Cap responded.

Pietro chose that moment to appear next to Wanda. He had been streaking through the city, leaving a trail of destroyed drones in his wake, and he was panting hard. "Okay," Clint said. "We need to—"

"Keep up, old man," Pietro said, and blurred away with his sister.

Hawkeye had vision unlike most people. He could see the blurring path of Pietro, and he could have...he caught himself weighing the balance of an arrow in his hand. "Nobody would know," he sighed. "Nobody."

But this was his new life, when he did the right thing, so Hawkeye just jogged after the twins.

CHAPTER 31

Iron Man hovered below the city. They were a long way up now, several miles and climbing. Friday was chasing data. "The antigravs are rigged to flip. Touch them and they'll go full reverse thrust," she said, displaying the trigger mechanisms.

Tony was sweating. This was bad and he wasn't figuring out how to make it good fast enough. "Spire's Vibranium," he muttered. "If Thor gave it a good whack..."

"A hit would crack it," Friday said, "but we're still talking global fallout."

"An energy seal. If we supercharge the other end, keep the atomic action doubling back . . ."

"That could vaporize the city," Friday said. "And everyone on it."

Tony kept sweating. "Make it shorter."

"Stark," Cap said over the comm. "What do you got?"

"Nothing great. There may be a way for me to blow up the city," Tony said. It was the best plan he had at the moment. "Keep it from impacting the surface. If you guys get clear . . ."

"I asked you for a solution, not an escape plan," Cap said.

"Impact radius is getting bigger every second," Tony said. "We're going to have to make a choice."

Cap broke the connection.

Solution, Tony thought. *Right.*

Natasha overheard the conversation between Cap and Tony. "Cap," she said quietly, "these people are going nowhere. If Stark finds a way to blow this rock . . ."

He shook his head, but she could see in his eyes that he knew they were losing. "Not until everyone is safe," he said.

"Everyone up here versus everyone down there? There's no math there," she said.

"I'm not leaving that rock while one civilian is on it."

"I didn't say we should leave," Natasha said. Soldiers in the midst of battle, they took a moment before the shooting started again. Over the edge of the city they saw a lot of sky and far below, the curving horizon of the Earth. "There are worse way stop go," Natasha added. "Where else am I going to get a view like this?"

It was the kind of thing you said when you thought you were going to die, and then Nick Fury had to ruin the mood by cutting in on the comm and saying, "I'm glad you like the view, Romanoff. It's about to get better."

A moment later the original Helicarrier loomed into view over the edge of the city.

"Nice, right?" Fury said. There was pride in his voice. "Pulled her out of mothballs with a couple of old friends. She's dusty, but she'll do."

"Fury, you son of a bitch," Cap said.

"You kiss your mother with that mouth?"

Cap couldn't help but grin. He heard Hill in the background, giving an altitude reading. They sure were way up in the air. Then another voice came over the comm, one

Cap didn't know. "Lifeboats secure to deploy. Disengage in three, two...take 'em out."

Wanda and Pietro appeared next to Cap as eight giant lifeboats fanned out from the Helicarrier and spaced themselves around the edge of the city. They were simple in shape, giant ferryboats with jet engines, and they were big enough to get a lot of Sokovians onto the Helicarrier fast.

"This is S.H.I.E.L.D.?" Pietro asked Cap.

Watching the Helicarrier, he said, "This is what S.H.I.E.L.D.'s supposed to be."

Pietro smiled, and Cap realized it was the first time he'd ever seen the kid smile without sarcasm or malice. This was just an ordinary, grateful smile. "This is not so bad," Pietro said.

Cap headed to meet the nearest lifeboat. "Let's load 'em up."

The Ultron drones headed for the lifeboats, but that turned out to be a good thing because it let the Avengers know where they needed to be ready to fight—except Thor, who once again had gone off somewhere, and nobody had seen the Vision in a while, either.

Another flight of drones headed for the Helicarrier. Cap heard Hill alert Fury to incoming bogeys, and heard Fury's calm reply. "Show 'em what we got."

That turned out to be War Machine, who streaked out of a hangar in the side of the Helicarrier and destroyed the first two before they knew he was there. "Now this is gonna be a good story," Rhodey said.

He was hit from behind and spiraled out of control for a moment before righting himself to see Iron Man right there with him. "Yep. If you live to tell it," Tony joked. Then they started working together, nice and easy, just as if they were fighting off Anton Vanko's robots back at the Stark Expo.

CHAPTER 32

Wanda seemed to be getting herself together, Clint thought, as she caught an Ultron drone in midair and tore it apart, all with little gestures of her hands and arms. Two more came in, trying to get at the lifeboat, but Clint and Wanda took them out, working together as if they were old partners.

All the uncertainty they'd felt a few hours ago on the Quinjet...it was gone. They were the Avengers again.

On the Helicarrier, Specialist Klein was reporting on the capacity of boat number six when Maria Hill looked up and shouted, "Incoming!"

A damaged Ultron drone smashed through the bridge windows straight at Fury. He dove out of the way as it crashed into a bank of instruments. Pieces of metal from both the drone and the consoles scattered across the bridge. The drone got up even though its legs were shattered and partly missing, still coming after Fury. Hill emptied her sidearm at it, and as soon as it was close enough, Fury himself finished it off, driving a broken spike of metal through its eye. It was going to take more than a kamikaze robot to knock him off his stride.

Ultron, irritated by the number of drones Thor was reducing to scrap, ambushed him and threw him into the ruins of the church. There, Thor found more of a fight than he'd expected. Ultron had Thor by the throat, and he had dropped Mjolnir. "You think you're saving anyone?" Ultron said. He held Thor with one hand and brushed the tip of one finger over the key that powered the spire assembly and the antigravity engines. "I turn that key and drop this rock a little early, and it's still billions dead. This key is the end of the world. Even you can't stop that."

Thor struggled in Ultron's grip, but he didn't try to break free. "I am Thor, son of Odin," he rasped, "and as long as there is life in my breast, I am running out of things to say, are you ready?"

Puzzled, Ultron blinked. "Huh?"

And that was when the Vision appeared again, with Mjolnir in his hand, taking a full-on home run swing that crushed Ultron up and out of the church, sending him flying over the smoking nearby buildings and out of sight.

Thor stood as Mjolnir returned to him. "It's terribly well balanced," the Vision commented.

"Well, too much weight and you lose power on the swing," Thor said. He liked this new artificial man, even if he found it strange that one such as the Vision should have been found worthy to wield Mjolnir. Thor trusted him, though. There were few men he would have trusted as partners in a deception such as the one they had just pulled on Ultron, but with the Vision he had no doubt. Mjolnir did not lie.

While target-shooting Ultron drones, Tony was also coming up with engineering plans and back-of-the-envelope calculations. "I got it," he said. "Create a heat seal. I could supercharge the spire from below." The idea was to figure something out that would spin the antigravity devices down without causing Sokovia to just fall out of the sky. The HUD simulation of damage now suggested that Sokovia falling from this altitude would reduce Europe to a pool of lava.

"Running numbers," Friday said.

Tony was momentarily distracted by an Ultron drone that destroyed one of the lifeboats' lift engines. He took the drone out and pushed the lifeboat back up to level so it could dock.

Friday had run her numbers. "A heat seal could work with enough power," she said.

"Thor, I got a plan!" Tony shouted.

"We're out of time," Thor answered. "Ultron's going for the core."

Undeterred, Tony said, "Rhodey! Get the rest of the people on board the Helicarrier! Avengers...time to work for a living."

He dove for the center of the city, where the church was, and where the key to the antigravity engines was...and where, if Ultron wasn't yet, he shortly would be again.

CHAPTER 33

Dozens of Ultron drones gathered around the church. Thor alone stood to oppose them. Then the Vision maneuvered into place, getting Thor's back. The drones charged into the ruins of the church, and Iron Man came screaming down, crushing the first row of them into the nearest building and then coming back around to land in front of the core.

Pietro, as usual appearing out of nowhere, made it four. Ultron himself reappeared, seemingly unharmed by the pounding he had already taken. He fired at the heroes, but Wanda batted aside the energy blast as she and Hawkeye entered. More and more drones closed in, and the Avengers shattered and melted and shorted them out. "Romanoff," Iron Man muttered, "you and Banner better not be—"

"Relax, shellhead," came her voice over the comm. "Not all of us can fly."

At that moment, she barged into the square outside the church...at the wheel of a snowplow. She used its huge blades to plow the drones out of the way, but as soon as she stopped in front of the church, they swarmed it. From inside the swarm, the Hulk appeared! Drones flew across the square, whole or in pieces. The Hulk was having the time of his life.

"What's the drill?" Natasha asked as she and the Hulk entered the church. Another wave of drones pursued them and tried to ambush them through other holes in the walls.

"This is the drill," Iron Man said, pointing at the core and the key at the center of its mechanism. "If Ultron gets a hand on the core, we lose."

If any one of them touched the core, Ultron would immediately transfer his consciousness to that one and set the city of Sokovia on a collision course with central Europe again. But the Avengers were there to stop that. Thor, flushed with the savage glee of the battle, saw Ultron himself landing in the square. Brandishing Mjolnir, he bellowed, "Is that the best you can do!?"

Ultron didn't answer at first. He hovered, holding up a hand, and the square around him filled with drones. The sky over his head filled with drones. Soon there were hundreds of drones massed for a final attack.

"You had to ask," Cap grumbled.

"This is the best I can do!" Ultron proclaimed. This is exactly what I wanted. All of you. Against all of *me*. How can you possibly hope to stop me?"

Iron Man nodded at Captain America, remembering their conversation a few days before. "Like the old man said. Together."

The Hulk stood in a gap in the wall and roared a challenge—and the drones attacked.

Waves of drones closed in on the nine Avengers, but they did not break. None of them could do anything but shoot or smash or melt or electrocute Ultron drones. It was a blur of shattered metal, sparking circuits, near misses... they worked together, in twos and threes when they needed the mutual support. They worked alone when there was no time to work together. They held the drones away from the core. They were a team. Above them, Ultron faced off with the Vision, who finally got the upper hand and flung Ultron down toward the stones of the square in front of the church.

Ultron hit, stumbled, got standing again. There was a pause as all the drones looked to their template, their Prime...

"All together now," Tony said. Thor stood in the church entrance. The Vision was off to one side, and Iron Man to the other. Lightning struck from Mjolnir out to Ultron's torso. Iron Man unleashed his chest beam, and the Vision blasted Ultron with the power of the jewel in his forehead. The three beams danced around one another, growing more and more intense until there was a powerful explosion that knocked them all back a step.

When the smoke cleared, Ultron was a sparking, shambling ruin of himself. He reminded Tony of how he had first appeared, at the party in Avengers Tower. Only this was worse. There were pieces falling off him, small fires burning in some of his motors... "You know," he said, "with the benefit of hindsight—"

He never got to finish. The Hulk stepped up and delivered an uppercut that sent Ultron rocketing for blocks over the empty buildings of Sokovia. Little pieces of him pattered down on the stones of the square. The remaining drones looked for a moment as if they might attack—but then they turned tail and disappeared.

"They'll try to get off the city," Thor said, whirling Mjolnir to take off and fly.

"Can't let them," Tony said. "Not even one."

Rhodey's voice came over the comm. "On it." He was patrolling the edge of Sokovia, along with a few of Fury's renegade agents who knew how to fly a Quinjet. "Who said you could leave?" he said as he blew a streaking drone apart with a missile barrage. Then he had another one lined up but out of nowhere came the Vision, who phased a fist into the drone's torso, then turned it solid again and tore the drone apart.

"Okay, what?" Rhodey said to no one. He hadn't been briefed on the new guy.

"Three minutes," Cap said into the comm. "Even I can tell the air is getting thin. You guys get to the boats. I'll sweep for stragglers. Be right behind you."

"What about the core?" Hawkeye asked.

"I'll protect it," Wanda said. She locked eyes with him, and he saw how far she had come already. "It's my job."

Clint nodded. "Nat?"

Together they took off for one of the boats.

Iron Man left to oversee his plan to build a heat seal around the spire, leaving Wanda to defend the core. A few stray drones attacked, but she didn't have any problem with them. Pietro arrived to take out a few more. "Get the people on the boats!" she yelled at her brother, irritated that he felt he always had to check up on her.

"No," Pietro said. "I'm not going to leave you here."

"I can handle these. You come back for me when everyone else is off, not before. You understand?"

"You know, I'm twelve minutes older than you," Pietro said.

She laughed. "Go!"

He went.

CHAPTER 34

Y"ou know what I need to do?" Hawkeye was driving toward the lifeboat with Natasha in the car. He was thinking about his last conversation with Laura. "The dining room. Knock out that east wall, make it a work space for Laura."

"You guys always eat in the kitchen anyway," Natasha commented.

Hawkeye nodded, skirting broken Ultron drones in the road. "No one eats in a dining room."

They passed the Hulk in a playground, tearing apart a

long-wrecked drone. Hawkeye knew what Natasha would want to do. "We don't have a lot of time," he said.

"So get your ass on a boat," she said, and got out of the car.

She approached slowly and carefully, keeping herself in the Hulk's field of view and making sure he looked at her a lot to maximize the chance that he would recognize her. "Hey, big guy," she said. "Sun's getting real low."

Hawkeye drove on and got to the boat, and he would have gotten off Sokovia no problem if it hadn't been for the little boy. There was a girl on the lifeboat, dazed and quiet, who suddenly snapped out of it when Clint came aboard and started shouting, "Costel! Costel!"

Clint heard an answering voice. Somewhere nearby. A small boy. He ran, found the boy, and took him back to the boat as Cap arrived with another small group of stragglers.

"Is that the last of them?" Thor asked.

"Yeah," Cap nodded.

"Then it's time," Thor said.

"Thor, I'm going to need you back at the church," Iron Man said. He was back below the city. He had cut his way into the bottom of the spire and was looking at the spinning mechanism. "You know...if this works, maybe we don't walk away."

"Maybe not," Thor said.

In the playground nearby, Natasha was just getting the Hulk calmed down enough that he would transform back into Bruce. It was a good thing she wasn't moving faster, though, because out of nowhere a hail of bullets hit the Hulk. He huddled over Natasha and looked up to see the Quinjet passing over their heads. Ultron was piloting it! They hadn't completely destroyed him. He was missing some pieces, and the ones he still had weren't in great shape, but he still functioned. The Hulk roared out a challenge.

The Quinjet came in low toward one of the lifeboats, where Cap, Thor, and Hawkeye were still leading the evacuation. When the next barrage started, Cap ducked down behind his shield and Thor wasn't afraid of a bullet, but Hawkeye? He wasn't an Enhanced, not really. He couldn't stop a bullet. All he could do was duck over this child, hide behind the car, and hope the boy lived. Also he hoped that Laura would know he had tried.

The Quinjet passed overhead, ending its strafing run... and Clint was alive. He opened his eyes and saw Pietro, standing where he had been. Pietro looked down at his wounds. They were bad. He glanced back at Clint. "You didn't see that coming," he said, and slowly sank forward onto the ground.

In the church, Wanda felt it. She screamed, and every Ultron drone within a hundred yards was shattered by the outpouring of her grief and pain.

The Hulk responded in his own way. He jumped up to the deck of the Helicarrier to leave Natasha there. She was wounded and barely conscious to see him go as he bounded away across the sky, back into the city. From there, he timed a leap that landed him on the rear ramp of the Quinjet.

A moment later, Ultron was ejected out the back of the Quinjet to fall toward the city, which still rose to meet him.

He landed hard on a tram near the church, crushing it.

Across town, Hawkeye started to notice something was wrong with him. He looked down and saw that Pietro wasn't the only one who'd been shot. Clint also had a hole, not too far from the patch of tissue he'd already had repaired. He sank down next to Pietro. "I'll be fine," he said to no one in particular. "Just been a long day."

Wanda was the first of the Avengers to get to where Ultron had landed. He tried to get up to meet her, but he was brutally damaged. She floated in the air near him. "If you stay here, you'll die," Ultron said.

"I just did," she said. "Do you know how it felt?"

She held a hand above his battered chest plate and

squeezed it into a fist. Different parts of Ultron began to crack and melt. He grunted and tried to speak but couldn't. Wanda flung her fingers wide, and his chest plate cracked open. Vibranium split like tinfoil. The main operating nodule that pulsed and sparked where a human's heart would be tore loose and flew into her hand.

"It felt like that," she said, as Ultron sputtered and sparked, slowly going silent.

CHAPTER 35

Inside the church, a heavily damaged drone dragged itself across the floor. No one was there to notice it...or to stop it as it got one arm up and turned the key in the core.

There was a series of clicks, and the core stopped spinning. The antigravity mechanism shut down, then reversed—and the city of Sokovia began to fall.

Tony Stark banged off the bottom of the stone projection around the spire. This was when he would find out whether his plan would work. Over the comm, the team was sounding off, gathering at the last lifeboat. The Vision had Wanda and was bringing her in. Everyone was accounted for…except Iron Man and Thor, who were underneath a million plus tons of stone as it plummeted back to Earth. It accelerated as Ultron's engines fired and drove it earthward at a speed that would destroy all life on the planet.

Tony planted himself at the base of the spire and fired his chest beam along its axis. The energy of the arc reactor spat and flared up the length of the spire. "Thor," he said. "On my mark."

Thor was already in the church. He thrust Mjolnir into the air and called down lightning such as the world had rarely seen. His body shook from the force and the pain of channeling it.

"Energy seal fusing," Friday said. "Ninety-eight percent…ninety-nine…"

If this didn't work, the entire upside-down mountain would collide with the Earth's surface again, acting just as a meteor would. The shock wave would liquefy the crust for miles around. Tsunamis would shatter coastlines all over the world. Enough dust and ash would kick up into the atmosphere that there wouldn't be a summer for twenty years. Crops would fail. Billions of people would die. Maybe all of them would die.

Only the Avengers could make sure that didn't happen. "Now!" Iron Man said.

Thor brought the hammer down onto the spire just as Tony cranked the suit's power up to overdrive, diverting every last bit of energy through the arc reactor. Beam and lightning and hammer all struck the spire at the same time—

—and a resonance spread through the Vibranium spire, quickly reaching a critical point—

—and the city of Sokovia exploded.

The rain of rubble spread over miles, but fell on empty countryside and the remote lakes of outer Sokovia. The Vibranium spire itself fell toward one of those lakes. Iron Man just barely got himself free of the spire. Thor was in the water, sinking. Tony would have to find him once the worst of the hailstorm was over.

Far above, the Hulk sat in the Quinjet, watching the ground recede. He looked around as Natasha appeared on the console readout. "Nice work, big guy," she said. "We did it. Job's finished. Now I need you to turn this bird around for me, okay?"

He watched her for a long time but did not answer.

"We can't track you in stealth mode," she said. "So help me out. I need you—"

He touched a button and the screen went blank. The Quinjet soared even higher.

On the Helicarrier, Natasha caught her breath. She remembered him saying *So . . . we just disappear?*

The last Ultron, bearing the scar on its faceplate from Captain America's shield, crept out of the crater that had once been the city of Sokovia and into the forest.

It stopped as the Vision floated down to land in front of it. "You're afraid."

"Of you?" Ultron's voice dripped contempt.

"Of death. You're the last one."

Some of Ultron's bravado drained away. "You were supposed to be the last. Stark asked for a savior and settled for a slave," he said.

The Vision considered this. "I suppose we're both disappointments."

Ultron had to laugh at this. "I suppose we are."

"Humans are odd," the Vision said. "They think order and chaos are somehow opposites and try to control what won't be. But there is grace in their failings. I think you missed that."

Ultron wasn't buying it. "They're doomed."

"Yes. But a thing isn't beautiful because it lasts. It's a privilege to be among them."

"You're unbearably naive," Ultron said, now smug and condescending again.

"Well," the Vision said. "I was born yesterday."

The forest lit up with the jewel beam's blinding flash as the last Ultron was destroyed.

CHAPTER 36

Tony Stark drove up to the New Avengers Facility, deep in the wooded hills of upstate New York. It was time to lower some profiles a little. They had work do to. Reconstruction. Healing. Team-building. He parked and went inside.

Maria Hill and Dr. Cho were leading individual groups developing new ops and scientific teams. Selvig had agreed to come aboard as a consultant on Asgardian research. Everyone was here but Barton, who was on an indefinite leave to get some home time with his new baby...and Bruce. Nobody knew where Bruce was. Tony walked through the facility's large open entryway and saw Natasha and Fury talking quietly upstairs.

She had just put her phone away after watching another video of the Bartons' new baby. Nathaniel Pietro Barton, fat and happy and well loved. Fury handed her a tablet with several blurry photographs on the screen.

"One of the tech boys tagged this. Splashed down in the Banda Sea," he said. "Could be the Quinjet. With Stark's stealth tech, we still can't track the damn thing."

"Right," Natasha said.

"Probably jumped out and swam to Fiji," Fury said. "He'll send a postcard."

"Wish you were here," Natasha said wistfully. Fury started to leave. "You sent me to recruit him, way back when. Did you know what would happen?"

She needed this answer, needed to know how much she had been manipulated and how much was real.

"You never know," Fury said. He was as gentle as he ever got. "You hope for the best. Then you make do with what you get. I got a great team."

"Nothing lasts forever," Natasha said. She could not remember ever feeling this sad.

"Trouble, Ms. Romanoff," Fury said as he walked away. "No matter who wins or loses, trouble still comes around."

He left her to her thoughts.

Cap, Tony, and Thor met in a hallway. "The rules have changed. We're dealing with something new," Tony said.

"An artificial life-form," Cap said.

Tony nodded. "A machine."

"So it doesn't count," Cap said.

Still nodding, Tony added, "It's not like a person lifting the hammer."

Amused, Thor looked on. "He can wield the hammer, he can keep the Mind Stone. It's safe with the Vision. And these days, safe is in short supply."

They nodded, but neither of them were quite ready to let go of wondering why the Vision could lift Mjolnir when they couldn't. "Okay," Cap said. "But if you put the hammer in an elevator—"

"It would still go up!" Tony finished. "Elevator's not worthy."

"I'll miss our little talks," Thor said.

"Not if you don't leave," Tony pointed out.

"I've no choice." Thor got more serious. "The Mind Stone is the fourth of the Infinity Stones to show up in the last few years. That's not a coincidence."

They walked outside together, and Thor finished his thought. "Someone has been playing an intricate game, and made pawns of us. Once all these pieces are in position..."

"Triple Yahtzee?" Tony suggested. Thor just looked at him. *Of course*, Tony thought. *Why would he know what Yahtzee is?*

"You think you can find out what's coming?" Cap asked.

"I do. Besides this one," Thor said, clapping Tony on the shoulder, "there's nothing that can't be explained."

Thor nodded at them and raised Mjolnir. In a prismatic column of light, he was drawn through a portal to...to wherever he was going. A burning Asgardian symbol was left on the grass.

"That man has no regard for lawn maintenance. I'm gonna miss him, though," Tony said. "And you're gonna miss me. There's gonna be a lot of manful tears."

Cap and Tony walked toward Tony's car, which started itself and drove to meet him.

"I will miss you, Tony," Cap said.

Standing in the open door of his car, Tony said, "Yeah,

but it's time for me to tap out. Maybe I should take a page from Barton's book. Build Pepper a farm, hope nobody blows it up."

"The simple life," Cap said.

"You'll get there one day."

"I don't know. Family, stability...the guy who wanted all that went into the ice seventy-five years ago. I think someone else came out."

"You're all right?" Tony asked. His concern was real.

Cap looked around at the new facility. There was a lot to do, and it was all worth doing. "I'm home," he said.

After Tony left, Cap found Natasha in the team locker room. "You want to keep staring at the wall, or you want to go to work?" He was sympathetic—she'd had a tough loss—but the Avengers still needed to know whom they could count on. "I mean, it's a pretty interesting wall..."

"I thought you and Tony were still gazing into each other's eyes," she cracked. "How do we look?" Just like that, the old Natasha was back in place, the all-business Black Widow.

Cap tossed her a tablet with a roster on it. She scrolled through it as they walked toward the training ground. "They're good," he said. "They're not a team."

"Then let's beat 'em into shape," Natasha said.

They walked into the Quinjet hangar. There, waiting, were War Machine, Falcon, the Vision, and Wanda Maximoff. They were eager, nervous, wondering what else they had to do to become part of the team. They turned to see Cap and Black Widow, who stopped just inside the door.

"Avengers," Captain America said. It was time for them to assemble again.

TURN THE PAGE FOR AN EXCITING PREVIEW OF
CAPTAIN AMERICA: THE FIRST AVENGER

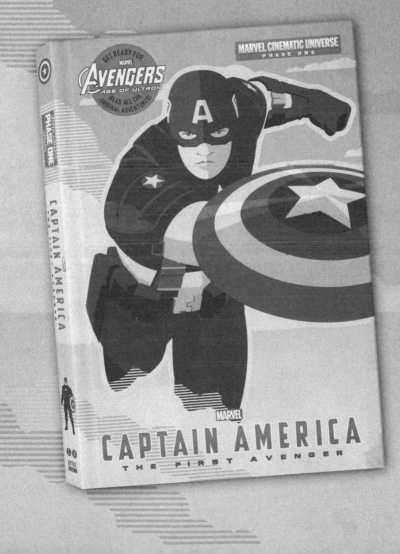

CHAPTER 1

Steve Rogers stood nervously in line at the recruitment center in Bayonne, New Jersey. Ahead of him, men stepped up one by one. And one by one, they got approved to join the army. Steve sighed and waited for his turn, which seemed as if it would never come. Looking around, he noticed several newspaper headlines about a brutal attack on a small Norwegian town that had left civilians hurt and homeless.

America was at war. Across the ocean, Europe was

full of gunfire and explosions. Men, women, and children were losing their lives and their homes as enemy forces invaded country after country. It had been going on for two years before America got involved, but then Pearl Harbor had happened. Now soldiers from the United States were flooding Europe, hoping to help the good guys win. But it wasn't going to be an easy—or a short—fight.

Steve felt the now-familiar rush of anger—and frustration. He wanted to be over there fighting more than anything in the world. But try as he might, he couldn't get past anyone in the recruitment centers, no matter how many attempts he made.

Steve had never been a big guy. Growing up on the streets of Brooklyn, New York, he and his best friend, James "Bucky" Barnes, had gotten into their fair share of fights. But it was usually Bucky who managed to keep them safe. Steve was scrappy, but physically he wasn't anything to write home about. He was skinny and frail, and because of his asthma, he couldn't even do enough exercise to add some muscles. He also had other health problems. The list was so long doctors usually thought he was making some of them up. But that was the last thing in the world Steve Rogers was going to do. He would have done anything to be fit for the army.

Not every soldier had to be a muscleman, like Johnny Weissmuller or Charles Atlas. You could win wars with brains and heart. Steve had enough brains, he figured, and he had a big heart. Some army recruitment center would eventually give him what he wanted most—a 1A stamp. Then he could be a US soldier, like his father had been. Which is why he now stood in line in the fifth recruitment center in the fifth city, hoping this would be the day. He knew it was not exactly legal to try to enlist in multiple locations, but so far, no one seemed to have caught on.

"Rogers, Steven?" a voice called out, startling Steve.

He stepped forward, wiping his hands nervously on his pants.

The doctor opened his file and began to scan it. "Father died of...?"

"Mustard gas," Steve said. He wasn't sad about it anymore. He was proud of his father's service, and he kept his head high as he said it. "He was with the One

Hundred and Seventh Infantry. I was hoping I could be assigned—"

"Mother?"

This one hurt a little more. "She was a nurse in a TB ward," Steve said. "Got hit. Couldn't shake it."

Not that anyone ever shook tuberculosis, not really. Steve had been an orphan for a while now. But he was doing all right on his own.

The doctor kept going through the file, his eyes growing wide as he took in all the ailments that had been checked off. The paper looked like it had been attacked by a red pen.

"Just give me a chance," Steve said.

"Sorry, son," the doctor said, looking up at him. "You'd be ineligible on your asthma alone."

He didn't say it, but Steve knew what he was thinking. *You're a fool, kid. The war is for strong men. Not for guys like you. Not for guys who can't even breathe right.*

"You can't do anything?" Steve asked anyway, hope in his voice.

"I'm doing it," the doctor answered. "I'm saving your life."

Then, as Steve watched, the doctor pulled out the dreaded stamp. With a resounding thunk, he pressed it down on the file, marking it with a big black *4F.*

Steve had failed—again.

A short while later, Steve was back in Brooklyn, inside a darkened movie theater. Up on the screen, images from the front lines flashed by in a newsreel. There was a picture of a bombed-out town, followed by images of soldiers pulling wounded men out of the line of fire. Another image showed the enemy marching into an undefended town, knocking down people and buildings as they went.

Nearby, Steve heard the unmistakable sound of someone crying. So many people had already lost loved ones or were about to send them off to the front lines. Steve didn't have anybody who would miss him if he went. His parents were gone, and his closest friend, Bucky, had already enlisted and was being shipped off the next day. Bucky would be over in Europe in no time, doing his part for the war effort, while Steve stayed behind. Useless.

The sound of an angry voice broke through Steve's

thoughts. "Who cares? Play the movie already!" someone shouted from behind him.

Steve's eyes narrowed. What kind of guy would say something like that at a time like this? He turned in his seat and tried to see who had spoken, but the screen had gone dark for a moment and it was difficult to make out anyone in the shadows. "Can you keep it down, please?" he asked quietly, hoping that the person with the bad attitude would hear him.

But apparently he didn't, because a moment later the guy called out, "Let 'em clean up their own mess!"

Steve shot out of his seat. He had had enough. "You want to shut up, pal?" he asked, turning around. Then Steve's eyes grew wide. In the light of the screen, he could now see who was talking. The guy was huge, and he looked way too eager to fight.

Steve gulped. What had he gotten himself into?

In the alley behind the theater, Steve stood with his fists in front of him. Balancing on the balls of his feet, he bobbed and weaved from side to side, trying to look tough. But the other guy was easily double his size, with fists the size of Steve's head.

The big guy advanced toward Steve, who leaped forward, hitting him with an uppercut and then getting a good punch into his kidney. The hit made the man flinch—but only for a moment. He came back at Steve, swinging his meaty fists. Steve ducked one punch and then another. He stepped lightly back and out of the way as the guy swung again. Smiling, Steve tried to get another hit in.

But then his luck ran out. He tried to punch the guy but got too close, and in one quick move, the big man knocked Steve flat with a roundhouse right. Steve got up and came after him again, and the big guy knocked him down again. This time Steve had a split lip. He spat blood on the alley bricks and got his guard up again.

"You just don't know when to give up, do you?" the big guy said.

"I can do this all day," Steve panted.